CW01203136

Sun, Sea & Boys

By
L.M. EVANS

L.M. Evans

Sun, Sea & Boys

Copyright

Copyright © 2019 by L.M. Evans
All rights reserved. No part of this publication may be reproduced, distributed, or transmitted in any form or by any means, including photocopying, recording, or other electronic or mechanical methods, without the prior written permission of the author, except in the case of brief quotations embodied in critical reviews and certain other non-commercial uses permitted by copyright law

For permission requests, write to the author, addressed "Request: Copyright Approval" at authorsgrant@gmail.com

This is a work of fiction. Names, characters, businesses, places, events, and incidents are either the products of the author's imagination or used in a fictitious manner. Any resemblance to actual persons, living or dead, or actual events is purely coincidental.
The authors are in no way affiliated with any brands, songs or musicians or artists mentioned in this book.

L.M. Evans

Sun, Sea & Boys

Contents

Copyright ___ iii
Contents ___ v
Dedication ___ vii
Acknowledgements ___ ix
Blurb ___ xi
Chapter One ___ - 13 -
  Free ___ - 13 -
Chapter Two ___ - 19 -
  Awkwardness ___ - 19 -
Chapter Three ___ - 26 -
  Memory Lane ___ - 26 -
Chapter Four ___ - 32 -
  The Rebel ___ - 32 -
Chapter Five ___ - 41 -
  The Boy Next Door ___ - 41 -
Chapter Six ___ - 50 -
  Pool Party ___ - 50 -
Chapter Seven ___ - 57 -
  The BBQ ___ - 57 -
Chapter Eight ___ - 66 -
  Surfing Lessons ___ - 66 -
Chapter Nine ___ - 73 -
  Sunsets and Sweet Goodbyes ___ - 73 -
Chapter Ten ___ - 80 -
  Regrets ___ - 80 -
Chapter Eleven ___ - 87 -
  Goodbye Summer ___ - 87 -
Chapter Twelve ___ - 93 -
  The Reunion ___ - 93 -
Chapter Thirteen ___ - 100 -
  New Neighbours ___ - 100 -

Chapter Fourteen	*- 111 -*
The Kiss	*- 111 -*
Author Bio	*- 120 -*
Contact Author	*- 122 -*

Sun, Sea & Boys

Dedication

This book is dedicated to two people, the first is my nan Jeanette. You are my guardian angel always shining bright when I need you.
Love you always
xx

This book is also dedicated to my daughter Alyssa, you have been nagging to read something I have written so, this one's for you.
XX

L.M. Evans

Sun, Sea & Boys

Acknowledgements

To my husband and children, I love you all. Thank you for letting me follow dream and to do what I thought was never possible.

Thank you to my parents for making sure I kept up with my school work when I was younger. To my sisters, family, and friends for supporting and believing in me, I love you all.

Being an indie author is scary there can be dark sides but also loads of good. If you are lucky enough to surround yourself with amazing people then you are truly blessed. I have made so many friends along the way since I began this journey. To those who started this crazy train with me and those who have hopped on board since I couldn't do this without your support it means so much. So, I want to say thank you to Debbie Williams, Mia Hudson, M.A Foster, Sienna Grant, Amy Davis, M.A Foster, Scarlet Le Clair, Phil Bruce, Lizzie James, Mike O Neill, Karen Hatton, Emma Lloyd, Leanne Colvin, Keira Garbett, Katie Jackson Georgina Hannan and Ellie Williams.

I also want to say a massive thank you to my editor Maria I don't know where I would be without you.

To my cover designer Mia Hudson

L.M. Evans

You had your work cut out for you with this one. Thank you for my amazing cover I fell in love with it the moment I laid eyes on it; it is absolutely bloody lush.

I want to say a special thank you to two women in particular; Debbie Williams and Mia Hudson we may be a million miles away but if it wasn't for you both I don't know where I'd be. You have both given me a kick up the ass when I was feeling down and I was ready to give up on writing. You two are amazing women and incredible writers and I am so grateful for everything you have both done for me.

Lastly, I want to say a massive thank you to all the bloggers who helped spread the word about my work.

Sun, Sea & Boys

Blurb

JC.

School is finally over and summer is here. Weeks filled with sun, sea, parties and cute boys, and spending time with her best friend Josie. This was the general plan before college starts in September.

What she didn't expect was to be shipped off for the summer to her Aunt Lucy's. Who she hadn't seen for a few years while her mother went on a cruise.

Colby Ryan.

Colby thought summer was going to be boring. They do the same thing every summer; Surf and sneak alcohol into pool parties.

His outlook changes when a cute girl arrives and is staying next door. Turns out she's his best friend's cousin and she's come to stay for the summer. The holidays are looking more fun by the minute.

Just when things are going good, fate steps in and knocks him off his feet.

L.M. Evans

This could turn into a summer of regrets.

Chapter One

Free

I open my eyes and smile. It's finally over. After five years in high school, I'm officially done. I picked my exam results up two days ago and now I have the rest of the summer to do whatever I want. Go to the beach, do sleepovers, or just stay in bed, until whenever I fancied getting up. I didn't need rush about, worry about homework and revising. Or have any teachers barking orders.

I push the duvet off me, roll over and grab my phone off my bedside table. Flicking the screen across, I unlock it with my fingerprint, then open up my Facebook app. I have a little red circle up in the right-hand corner indicating I have thirty notifications. Clicking on the circle, the tab scrolls down so I flick through them. A few birthdays, some photos that been shared and a invite to a party or BBQ. I click on the invite and notice that it's my friend Paige, who is organising it, with her older brother, while her parents are on a cruise. I acknowledge that I'm attending, then close the app and shut off my phone, before placing it back on my bedside table.

Swinging my legs over the edge, I stand up and make my bed. Nothing is going to sour my mood; I am so freaking happy. I walk over to my wardrobe and pull out a pair of black leggings and a white tank top, then throw them onto my bed. Before grabbing a clean bra and knickers from the drawers and adding them.

Opening my bedroom door, I stroll across the landing to the bathroom, and turn on the shower. I strip out of my pyjamas and climb in. Squirting some shampoo into the palm of my hand, I scrub my hair, before rinsing it out. I then begin washing the rest of my body with shower gel.

Twenty-five minutes later, I'm finished in the shower. I wrap a towel around my body and a second towel around my hair. Walking out of the bathroom, I notice my mums bedroom door is open and her bed is made, she must have got up while I was in the shower. I continue across the landing to my bedroom and close the door. After drying my body, I change in to my bra and knickers then put my leggings on and finally my tank top. Grabbing my hair dryer, I plug it in by the side of my bed, unravel the towel on my head and start drying my hair. After fifteen minutes my hair is dry and I pull it back into a messy bun, before grabbing my phone and heading downstairs for breakfast.

"Hey honey, how did you sleep?" Mum asks as I grab the cereal and a bowl out of the cupboard.

"Amazing mum, schools finished and I'm free to do whatever I want over the summer, before college starts in September"

She smiles, but it doesn't quite reach her eyes like it normally would, she pauses while making her cup of coffee.

"JC, I wanted to talk to you about the summer. Now I know you were making plans now that school is over with your friends, but I need a break away. So, I am going on a cruise with some friends. You are going to stay with your Aunt Lucy, Uncle Steve, and your cousins. It will be for the full summer, until college starts up in September. I think you'll have fun with your them…."

I don't give her the chance to finish. "Mum, I don't want to go to Aunt Lucy's, I haven't spoken to them for ages. I don't even talk to Trixie or Zeke on Facebook," I reply angrily

"JC, I'm doing this, you are sixteen and live under my roof. So, you will do as you are told and right now, I am telling you that you are going to stay with your Aunt and Uncle. Your Aunt is the only living relative of your fathers and she wants to spend time with you. So, stop acting like a five-year-old and suck it up, you're going and that's the end of it."

"Fine, I hate you mum. I can't believe I have to spend the summer with people I hardly know. It's not fair…"

Slamming her cup on the counter and spilling its contents, she spins around to face me.

"No JC, what is not fair is seeing someone you love die. It killed me watching your father die. Grow up and start acting your age. Then go pack a suitcase and whatever else you want to take with you. They will be here tomorrow to pick you up." Mum orders, before turning around to carry on pottering in the kitchen.

I don't bother eating the rest of my breakfast, slamming my spoon on the side, before storming back up the stairs. Banging my bedroom door closed.

"JC if you keep acting like the way you are, I will send you to live with your Aunt permanently." Mum shouts

My phone rings, looking at the screen I find it's my best friend Josie. I swipe across the screen to answer.

"Hello," I say, before throwing myself on the bed.

"JC, you are not going to believe this. Symon Davies the most popular boy in school, is throwing a massive UV paint party. His parents have hired the old community centre hall out, as a celebration for finishing school. Everyone is invited. It's going to be amazeballs; we have to go shopping for new outfits to wear," she excitedly shouts down the phone.

"Josie, chill already, I'd hate to burst your happy bubble, but I can't go." I say, but she cuts me off.

"What. Why? You have to come; I need my girl with me. You know that Symon's friend Craig will be there. Plus, you know how long I have had a crush on him," she whines.

I know she's had a massive crush on Symon since he strutted in to our class the first day of high school. He's had all the girls drooling over him apart from me. I had a crush on his best friend Craig.

"Josie, you know I would love to come party with you, but I can't. My mother is sending me to go stay with my Aunt for the summer. You know how my mother gets once she has her mind set, there is no changing it. I promise we will FaceTime each other and call. When I get back, we can have a sleepover before we start college in September." I say, offering a compromise.

"JC, it won't be the same without you gone all summer. Do you swear you will call me a few times a week, as well as Face Timing?"

"I swear, I will. I'd better go, I have a lot of packing to do." I reply, before hanging up.

I drag my suitcase from under my bed and throw it on the top, before unzipping it and start packing my clothes and shoes. It takes me a good hour to get everything I want to take. I am standing on the chair in the middle of my wardrobe looking for a few books, when my phone starts ringing. Climbing down with the books after finding them, I drop them by my suitcase and answer the call.

"Hello."

It's Josie again, this girl just won't take no for an answer.

"JC, have you finished packing yet?" Can you come to the park for a few hours to hang out?" She begs.

"Josie, I literally just finished, I was looking for my Abbi Glines books on top of my wardrobe."

"Does that mean your free to come hang out with us?"

"Wait Josie, who is us?"

"Oh umm…" she hesitates before continuing "Symon, Craig and me." she replies excitedly.

"Josieee. You know I muddle my words when I'm nervous around Craig."

"Pleaseee come on, I won't see you all summer, I'll come to your house and beg on my knees until you say yes."

"Okay fine, give me ten minutes so I can change and I'll meet you at the end of the street" I tell her before hanging up.

I quickly add my three Abbi Glines, Sea Breeze Series books to my suitcase, before zipping it up and standing it by my bedroom door for the morning. I then change from my leggings to my denim jean shorts and leave my tank top on. I slip my feet into my sandals, grab my bag with my purse and front door key in, and throw it over my shoulder. Then get my phone from the bed and head downstairs. Mum is in the living room watching TV. She turns as she hears me approaching.

"Have you finished packing?"

"Yes mum, I packed my suitcase. Josie asked me if I can hang out with her for a few hours." I tell her, *but what I really wanted to say is she spoilt my summer plans.*

"Okay good. As long as your suitcase is packed for the morning you can go out, but I want you back by nine-thirty and no later." She orders.

I agree then head out.

Chapter Two

Awkwardness

Josie is sat on the wall at the end of the street, with her head down, typing on her phone when I reach her. She looks up and smiles.

"OMG JC, Symon just text me, he wants us to go over to his house and chill out." She beams with excitement, then jumps down from the wall.

"Josie, I don't fancy playing the third wheel tonight, I have enough to deal with…."

"Babe, you won't be the third wheel, Craig will be there as well and I know he is dying to talk to you."

She grins like she knows something I don't.

"Josieee, what aren't you telling me?" I ask, but she ignores my question. Looping her arm through mine, she pulls me along with her.

"Josie, fine we can go to Symon's, but please don't leave me alone with Craig okay, or I'm going to go home." I say with a serious face.

"I promise," she says, lifting her pinkie finger. "Pinkie promise."

We snap our little fingers together and shake them.

Twenty minutes later, we are walking up the path to Symon's front door. Josie knocks the door and a few seconds later he opens it, wearing black shorts, a white tank top and bare feet.

"Hey girls come in; we are in the dining room." He explains as we walk in, then motions for us for follow him, after closing the front door.

We walk through the long, stark white, hallway, that has a dark wooden floor, until we come to a small room. Upon entering, I notice a black, corner sofa and a forty-two-inch LED, black TV on the wall. Craig is sat on the far end of the sofa with a can of coke in one hand and his phone in the other. Glancing up when we walk in the room.

"Girls, you know my boy Craig, right? I think you had a few classes together when we were in school." Symon explains.

"Hey Craig, I'm Josie and this is JC," Josie introduces us.

He smiles, "Hey girls, come sit down," he motions with his hand.

"Thanks," we both say as we walk over to the sofa.

"So, what are you boys up to?" Josie asks them.

"Not much, just watching TV and catching up. What about you girls, any plans for the summer? "Symon asks.

"Well, I will be going to a few parties and just chilling out." Josie replies.

"What about you JC?" Craig asks.

"I... um," I stammer nervously.

"JC will be staying with her Aunt for the summer." Josie finishes for me. I smile, a silent thank you at her.

"Aww man that sucks, you'll miss all the fun. There's a paint party, the last week of August, happening in an old circus tent. At the old school grounds. Also, there's a ton of parties happening, it's going to be a wild summer." Symon replies, before fist pumping Craig's hand.

"Symon, can I use your bathroom please?" Josie asks.

"Sure, it's up the stairs, second door on the left," he explains.

Once she's left the room, Symon switches to the music channel on the TV, then turns to me.

"So, JC, a little bird told me your secret ..." he pauses taking in my reaction.

My heartbeat accelerates, my breathing heightens, and suddenly I feel very nervous. Josie must have told him I had a crush on Craig.

"I was wondering if it's true about who you have a crush on?" he asks.

Yep, I want the floor to swallow me whole. Symon smirks and flicks his head towards Craig. Who is oblivious to the conversation that's happening. I nod my head, just as Josie comes back downstairs.

"What did I miss?" She asks and glances as me. I seriously want to throttle her. She knows the girl code rules and yet she still blabbed to Symon as soon as he made goo, goo eyes at her.

"Nothing much, want to play spin the bottle?" he asks and we all agree. Sitting on the floor in a circle, Symon spins the bottle first and it lands on Josie.

"Josie, truth or Dare?" He asks her and she picks a dare.

"I dare you to kiss Craig with tongues, for two minutes." he tells her.

Josie gets up moving the bottle to the side and cups Craig's face, kissing him hard, then stops.

"That was too easy. My turn," she says before spinning the bottle and it stops on Craig. "Come on then hot stuff truth or dare?" she asks and he picks truth. "Who was your first school crush?".

"That's easy, it would be Mrs May, our French teacher, she was smoking hot," he replies, before spinning the bottle where it lands on me.

I'm given the option of truth or dare, and I picked dare.

"Okay JC, I dare you to straddle Symon's lap and kiss him, tongues and all, for four minutes."

I get up nervously and walked over to Symon, where he grabs my legs, so my knees are either side of him and I end up on his lap. He then grabs my ass, squeezing it hard.

"Kiss me, doll face," he says, before leaning forward and sticking his tongue in my mouth.

My heart begins to race, my body gets hotter.

"Okay, that's enough you two," Josie shouts.

She sounds annoyed, I can tell by her voice. It wasn't my fault, it's not like I wanted to kiss Symon. Besides, she made out with Craig and she knows how much I like him.

I climb off him, sit back down and spin the bottle. This time it lands on Symon.

Picking truth, I ask, "You are a chicken, okay fine, who do you fancy that was in our year, at school?"

"Rayleigh, she was stunning as hell," he answers, then spins the bottle, this time it's landed on Craig, where he picks dare.

"I dare you to pick JC up, throwing her over your shoulder and take her to my spare room. Get some fresh cream, squirt it over her body and lick it off. Oh, and we want pics."

I quickly scramble to my feet.

"No way, not happening. Game over, I can't do that," I start to protest, but Craig gets up with a wicked glint in his eyes.

"Oh, I think not sweetheart, the fun is just beginning."

He walks towards me, like an animal that wants to play with its prey, before he eats it. I screech, then dodge him and slip out the room. I run towards the front door, but he's too fast, catching up to me. He cages me in against the front door, sporting a massive grin on his face

"Craig please?" I beg."

"JC, I'm only joking," he says, then stands up straight, just as Symon and Josie come to find us.

"Sy, games over, you're scaring JC. Let's just stick a film on and order food later, okay...?"

Symon agrees, but I can see Josie is pissed off. We all go back to the dining room, where Symon puts on the film Jupiter Ascending. We all settle in to watch the movie, Craig pulls me closer to him and puts his arm around my shoulder. I glance over at Josie and Symon, and notice they are holding hands.

"JC, I'm sorry about before, Symon thought it be fun, but we took things a bit too far. I hope you can forgive me?" Craig whispers.

I gaze into his eyes.

"I do, but don't do that again, promise?"

He agrees and turns back to the film. I place a kiss on his cheek, as a thanks. Near the end of the film, a pizza arrives, I had no idea Symon had ordered it. We eat the pizza and watch the rest of the film.

After it has ended, we start talking, then my phone starts ringing, it was my mum. I glance up at the clock it's twenty past nine.

"Shoot I'm going to be late."

I swipe the screen and answer.

"Hello. Yes mum, I'm sorry I lost track of time. Yes, I am on my way now," I tell her and hang up.

I glance across to Josie who has nodded off on the sofa. I'm torn on what to do, Symon notices my inner turmoil.

"JC, I'll make sure she gets home, have you got a lift?"

I shake my head. "No, we walked here, so I am going to walk back, can you tell her I'll phone her." I say as I walk to the front door and Craig follows.

"I'll walk you home, "he says and we leave.

As we approach my house, I stop and turn to Craig.

"Thanks for walking me home."

"My father always told me make sure my date gets home before I do. Too many weirdos about. Have a good summer JC, maybe I can take you out when you get back?" he asks.

"Sure, I'd like that. Goodnight Craig," I say and kiss him on the cheek, before walking up to my house and go inside

Chapter Three

Memory Lane

I'd set my alarm, the night before, so I could wake up early, and have a shower before my Aunt arrived. It's almost nine o'clock in the morning, and I've already had breakfast.

Sitting on my bed, I was reading my book, The Bet .by Rachel Van Dyken to pass time. Rachel was one of my favourite authors. I've read this book loads of times, and it never gets old. The things the Gran character gets up to in the story cracks me up. She's sneaky, matchmaking the characters and the things she comes out with, are so freaking funny. It's one of the funniest books I have ever read. I was about to start a new chapter when the doorbell chimes. I glance at the clock and it's quarter past nine in the morning.

"JC, your Aunt is here." Mum shouts up the stairs.

I grab my gym bag, toss my charger and headphones in, along with my purse. I slip my feet into my sandals then throw the strap of my gym bag over my shoulder. Then pick up the book I was reading, shoving it under my arm. I grab my suitcase, carry it out the door and downstairs. Before dropping it by the front door, along with my gym bag. Lucy and mum are sat on the sofa when I walk in the living room. They both look up when they notice me.

"Hey sweetie, are you ready to spend the summer with us?" Lucy asks. I put on a fake smile.

"Yeah it's going to be fun. Where is Uncle Steve? "I ask.

"He's at home with the kids. I said I would come on my own to pick you up, so we can catch up on the drive back down. Have you got everything, hair brush, toothbrush, mobile phone?" she asks.

"Shoot I forgot my phone and toothbrush," I say and rush back upstairs to grab them. When I come back down, mum is wiping away tears and hugs Lucy.

"Everything okay?" I ask them both.

"Yes, everything is all good, come on I want to hit the road now to avoid traffic." My Aunt says.

We put my case and gym bag in the boot of the car, then I hug mum goodbye and promise to call. She hands me a small white envelope.

"JC, this is for you, it's three hundred pound from your trust fund. Don't go mad with it and enjoy your summer." She says before I climb in the car.

We are an hour into the journey, when Aunt Lucy turns the radio down.

"JC sweetie, I know you aren't happy about spending the summer with us…" She pauses taking in my reaction before continuing "But I wanted you to spend time with us. Your cousins are looking forward to seeing with you. It will be an amazing summer JC."

"Thanks Aunt Lucy, I'm just nervous because I haven't stayed with you since I was ten-years-old. Plus, we haven't really spoken much…"

"JC hunny, I know we haven't spoken much over the last few years. It was hard losing my brother; your dad and I struggled. You are so much like him, but we love you so much sweetie. We are blood and that will never change Okay. I'm going to be honest with you. Recently I was sorting the attic out and I found a box of stuff that your father had me keep for him. I was going through it and found a letter he had written; in case anything should happen to him. He wanted me to make sure you had fun before you start college, and I want to keep that promise."

She wipes a tear from her eye with one hand and then turns the radio back up. I gaze out the passenger window before closing my eyes.

I must've fallen asleep, because the next thing I feel is my Aunt shaking my arm to wake me up.

"Hey sweetie, we are here." she says turning the engine off before climbing out the car. I unbuckle my seatbelt, open the car door, and step out taking in my surroundings. The car was parked on the drive outside a big house, with a massive front garden. I turn around taking in the neighbouring houses, all of them look the same. Only difference being, some have a full gardens and no drive. The front door opens and Uncle Steve comes out to greet us, he gives Aunt Lucy a kiss and walks over to me.

"JC, how was the drive? It's good to have you stay with us for the summer," he says, not giving me a chance to reply to his question, and gives me a big bear hug.

"Steve let the girl breathe, she fell asleep on the way here and only just woke up. You're probably overwhelming her."

He lets go and walks around me to get my suitcase and bag out of the car boot.

"It's all good, I'm fine," I tell my Aunt, smiling to reassure her.

"Where are the kids?" She asks Steve.

"They've gone to the beach with some friends." Steve replies.

"Beach? I ask.

He grins," Lucy, didn't tell you?" he asks me and I shake my head in response. "We are fifteen minutes from the beach. Your cousins spend most of the time down there with their friends." he replies, before taking my suitcase and bag into the house.

"Come on, let's show you to your room. Zeke has moved to the attic for now, so his old room is going to be yours for the summer." Lucy replies before locking the car and walking up to the house.

I follow her in, and take in everything around me. The house has a big, open plan living room, with dining room with dark brown, wooden flooring. A large black, corner sofa sits in the one corner and a massive forty-two-inch TV is on the wall above a white fireplace. A old log burner sits in the centre of it. On the other side of the room is a black glass, dining table and six white, leather chairs.

"JC, follow me and I'll show you your room." Lucy says.

So, I follow her up the black carpeted stairs to the first room on the landing. She opens the door revealing a single bed with the new York skyline on the duvet cover. Black walls with a silver border along it and Chinese writing up the top in silver. A small twenty- four-inch TV is sat on the white chest of drawers, with a small DVD player. By the side of it is a tall white wardrobe. My suitcase is stood by the side of the bed with my bag. I walk in and look out the window, I can see the whole of the back garden and the neighbours gardens either side.

"I'm going to leave you unpack, I have made a nice chicken curry for dinner. Your mum said you love chicken curry, so I will heat that up for us all later." She says before closing the door leaving me on my own. I sit down in the bed and my phone beeps, its Josie.

Have a good summer see you when you get back.

I reply back.

Sun, Sea & Boys

Summer is going to suck. Miss you.

Chapter Four

The Rebel

After forty minutes of unpacking, I grab my book, continue reading. I was in a fit of giggles when someone knocks on the door,

"Come in."

A girl with a black pixie haircut and glasses, pokes her head around the door, it's Trixie my cousin.

"Oh my... JC... I... ran as... soon ... as mum phoned me. I run… all the way home. I can't believe your here for the summer." She says, while panting.

I smile, close my book, then swing my legs over the edge of the bed and sit up.

"Hey Trix, how are you?"

Next thing I know, she runs over before launching herself at me, giving me a hug.

"JC, I missed you, it's been years since we see each other. So good to have another girl around, you look good.

How have you been? Do you have a yummy boyfriend back home?" she bombards me with questions.

"I'm good and no I don't have a boyfriend back home. What about you, do you have a boyfriend? I ask.

"I don't, but there is a boy I like. He's cute and he's super sweet …"

Next thing I know there is a deep, masculine voice cutting her off.

"Hey dork, mum told you to leave JC to rest."

Zeke is leaning against the door frame, in black surfer shorts and a tank top on. I open my mouth to reply, but my eyes are met with stunning blue eyes, a boy with jet black hair, wearing dark blue, surfer shorts with no shirt He's standing beside Zeke, and smirks at my reaction. I feel like I have butterflies in my stomach, I just can't take my eyes off him.

"Z, go back to your bat cave in the attic and take your fan club with you," she spits back.

"Whatever dork, nice to see you JC. Come on dude, let's leave these two to catch up." he says to his friend and then they both disappear.

"Summer is going to be awesome with you here. We are going to have so much fun and I think you have an admirer," Trix says grinning.

"What…. him …no way." I reply

"Oh yes, the way, Colby was staring at you. I'd say it was crush at first sight," she giggles and we both fall back on the bed.

"Trix, who is he, anyway?"

"Well is name is Colby Ryan, he's the same age as us. He's been Z's best friend since primary, they are as thick as thieves when they are together. He also split up with his girlfriend Natalia a few months back and he's currently single. Do you fancy him? Because I think he fancies you" she says.

"What. No... no. Okay let's change the subject." I can feel myself blushing and bury my head in the pillow.

"Oh my god, you do." She shouts.

"Hey dork, keep the noise down, I can hear you up here," Zeke yells.

Trix giggles, "Mind your own business Freak" she yells back.

"Don't worry, your secret is safe with me," she whispers.

We spent the last few hours catching up and before long Aunt Lucy is calling us down for food.

We are all sat around the table together, while Aunt Lucy serves the curry. She also invited Colby to stay, which he accepts.

"You girls sound like you were having fun with all the giggling coming from JC's room." Uncle Steve says smiling, before placing some food in his mouth.

"Oh, leave them alone Steve, they are making up for lost time," Aunt Lucy tells him. "How are you settling in sweetie, are you unpacked?" she asks.

"Yes, all unpacked."

"JC, do you have a boyfriend back home?" Zeke asks.

"Zeke. Don't go asking your cousin personal questions like that." Aunt Lucy tells him off.

"What? I was only asking as my boy fancies her" he says as Colby starts coughing. Zeke slaps him on the back. Then looks at me with a wicked grin.

Little sod, I thought he had heard our conversation earlier.

"Zeke, you can wash and dry for being so rude." Uncle Steve tells him.

"Dad, that's not fair, I was only asking a question…"

Uncle Steve cuts him off. "Keep talking and you will be grounded for the summer," he threatens, Zeke gives up and finishes his food.

Finishing my meal, I let my Aunt know I've enjoyed it.

"Aunt Lucy that was really nice, thank you. I am stuffed."

"Your welcome sweetie, if you and Trixie are finished, why don't you go hang out down the beach?"

"That's an awesome idea, mum. JC, do you have a swimming costume?" Trix asks.

"I have my two piece."

We leave the table to go change and grab a towel from upstairs.

Twenty minutes later we are both changed and have bags for the beach. When we come back downstairs the boys are in the kitchen, Aunt Lucy and Uncle Steve are sat on the sofa, watching TV.

"Hey mum, we are going now, catch you later," Trixie says.

"Okay honey, you girls have fun" she shouts over her shoulder.

We head out the door, before we reach the end of the drive, Zeke shouts.

"Hey dork, wait up, we are going for a surf, so we will walk with you."

I glance back to where Zeke's voice came from. He and Colby are both walking towards us with surf boards under their arms.

"I didn't know you could surf," I say to Zeke as he approaches. He swings his arm over my shoulder.

"I been surfing for as long as I could swim, pretty much. Colby's older brother Ross taught us both, you should see him when he's riding the waves, he's amazing…"

Trixie cuts him off. "Aww does Z have a crush on Ross?" she teases.

"Hey dork, I'm not the one who's crushing on someone."

"Shut up Freak, come on JC, let's get away from these two." Trix says, pulling me out from under Zeke's arm.

We walk little faster than the boys, when Trixie slows her pace, I ask her about Zeke's comment earlier.

"Trix, what did Zeke mean by his comment earlier about crushing on someone older?" I ask.

"Let's get to the beach and I'll tell you."

Not long after we arrive, Trix walks over to a spot, pulls out her towel and I follow her doing the same, placing it on the sand beside hers. We both kick off our flip flops and stretch out on the sand. Just as we get settled, the boys walk by, dumping the towels, they both had tucked in the backs of their shorts, next to us. Before continuing down to the sea and sit on their surfboards.

"So, JC, you know the question you asked about that boy? It's Colby's brother Ross, he's nearly twenty. He's so cute, but he just sees me as the sister of his brothers best friend," Trixie explains.

"Aww, Trixie. Does he live far from you?" I ask.

"He lives next door, but he's away at the moment."

"Let's forget about boys for the summer and have some fun." I smile at her, "Do you fancy going in the sea?"

Trix agrees, so we take our shorts off and walk down to the shore. The cold-water splashes against our legs the deeper we go.

"Oh my god it's so cold."

"I'm used to it..." She's cut off when Zeke and Colby paddle over to us.

"You girls fancy coming on the boards with us?" Zeke asks.

"No way, I remember last time. JC can if she wants, I want to go and catch some sun." Trixie says before turning around, backing out of the water, and walking up to where our towels were.

"What do you say JC, do you want to try and learn to surf?" Colby asks.

"I'm not sure, I've never been on a surfboard before."

Colby and Zeke both paddle closer.

"Hey cuz, you're in safe hands I promise. I'll go put my board on the sand and we can use Colby's board," he says as he paddles back to shore.

"Why don't you climb up here with me and we can teach you the basics?" Colby says, but Zeke cuts in as he swims back to us.

"I don't think so pal," he says then shoves Colby off the board.

A few seconds later he pops up from the water flicking his head back and wipes the water out of his face.

"Dude, not cool," he says leaning his arms on the board.

Zeke grabs me around the waist picking me up, then places me on Colby's surfboard.

"Oh my god Zeke, I'm going to fall," I yell, squeezing Zeke's shoulders tightly as he floats beside the surf board.

"Will you retract the claws and put your legs either side of the board, then you won't fall." He orders.

I do as he says and put my legs down, but I still feel wobbly. So, I squeeze his shoulders.

"I'm scared I'm going to hit my head and fall off."

Colby places a hand on my bare skin.

"JC, I promise you, I will not let you hurt yourself." he says as Zeke moves my hands that currently have a death grip on his shoulders, and places them onto the surfboard. He shuffles back a little, so I can't go back to squeezing him.

"Zeke please don't leave me on here, I don't feel safe…"

Next thing I know Colby is moving me forward a little

"I'm going to fall," I screech.

There is a splash from Zeke ending up in the water and Colby is sat on the surfboard instead, he starts kicking his feet and the board moves away from Zeke.

"Dude, you're not funny get down and come back before you get her hurt." Zeke shouts with concern.

"Z, she safe, don't worry, go check on Trix, you a really annoyed her earlier." Colby shouts back.

"Fine, but no funny business. I got my eye on you," Zeke says before getting out the water, grabbing his surfboard and makes his way up the beach to where Trixie is.

Colby wraps both his arms around me pulling me tight against his chest, I freeze. I've never been in close contact like this with a boy before.

"JC, you okay?"

"Y... yeah I'm just nervous."

He stops kicking his feet and the surfboard just floats on the water.

"JC, can you look at me for a second?"

I do as he asks and shift nervously so I can look at him. He moves slightly to the right so he can see my face better. Lifting his right hand, he cups the left side of my face.

"JC, I promise you are safe with me. I've been surfing for a long time and like Zeke said earlier, we learned from the best, my brother Ross... He's won surfing competitions in Australia and a few in the UK. Please trust me okay?"

I nod, "Okay Colby" I say.

He leans forward and kisses me on the nose, before dropping his hand and turning back around. We start moving across the water again.

Chapter Five

The Boy Next Door

I don't know why, but after being sat so close to Colby on the surfboard for a good few hours, I have this feeling. It's like nothing I've felt before. When he's close by or touches my skin, I feel giddy. My heart begins to race and my legs feel like jelly, but when I gaze into his eyes, it feels like I am hypnotized and frozen to the spot.

It was getting dark by the time we get back to the house. Zeke dumps his surfboard at the side of the house, before going over to Colby's house next door. As we walk through the door, Uncle Steve looks up.

"Did you girls have fun today?"

"Yeah it was awesome, the boys tried teaching JC to balance on the board." Trixie replies.

"How was it JC?" he asks.

"It was okay, scary at first, but the boys think they will get me surfing by the end of the summer break."

"Dad, where is mum?" Trix asks her father.

"She was tired, so I sent her up to bed early at seven." He explains, then goes back to watching some animal documentary on the TV.

"I'm going to order takeaway from Pizza Hut, any preference?" he asks us.

"BBQ chicken pizza." Trixie replies then glances as me. "That okay with you? It is lush, best pizza you will ever have." she adds. I smile at her

"Sounds good to me."

"Pizza it is, Trixie can you go ask your brother what he wants and then I'll order."

She does as her father asks and sends Zeke a text, within minutes he replies. He wants the same as Trixie suggested.

We leave Uncle Steve to go upstairs to our rooms, I was about to go in the shower when Trixie comes in.

"Dad said food will be about an hour and Colby invited us to go next door to hang out," she says keeping her voice low.

"Oh, should I change?" I ask and she shakes her head.

"No stay as you are. The Ryan's have a pool in the back garden. My dad helped build it two years ago before their dad left for no reason, but I heard mum and Mrs Ryan talking and he was sleeping around and moved in with the other woman," she explains.

We both walk downstairs and head next door, walk through the side gate and around the back. The pool wasn't massive like the ones you seen on TV white tiles around the inside on the medium-sized rectangular pool on the middle of a patio garden. Zeke was currently doing laps and Colby was sat on the side of the pool. He looks up when he hears us approaching.

"Hey girls," he smiles. Trixie drops her towel on the patio chair then runs and jumps in the pool. A few seconds later she pops up spluttering.

"Hey dork," Zeke says before dunking her under. The sound of the doors opening behind me makes me look. A tall blonde girl steps out with a boy that looks like an older version of Colby.

"Hey bro, I thought you weren't due back for a few days?" Colby says, getting up from the side of pool and walks over to him, then does that weird hug thing that boys do.

"JC, this is Ross, my brother. Ross this is JC she is Z's and Trix's cousin, she's here for the summer," he explains.

Ross holds his hand out and I shake it.

"Nice to meet you sweet cheeks, this is Nicole a good friend of mine. Nic, this is Colby, my little brother, and his friend JC. The two in the pool are a Trix and Zeke they live next door." Ross says introducing us.

I glance in the pool and Trixie's expression changes from carefree and happy, to sour, the moment she sees Nicole. I drop my towel on the chair where Trixie's is and sit on the side of the pool, with my feet dangling in the water. Trix swims over to me.

"You okay?" I ask her knowing how she feels about Ross.

"Yeah, I'm fine. He can do whatever he wants, he's free and single. Also, he doesn't see me the way he sees other girls." she says as Colby and Ross join me by the side of the pool and Nicole sits on one of the chairs.

Trixie swims off as Ross sits beside me and starts doing laps.

"Something I said?" he asks. I shrug, I know exactly why she's annoyed and if Ross opened his eyes he would too.

"Ross, my man when did you get in?" Zeke says, as he makes his way over to where we all are. These two are like two old women exchanging stories. Ross was telling Zeke about his latest surfing competition, and Zeke was hanging off every word Ross says. After a few minutes I lean forward and dive into the pool and start doing laps with Trixie. I'm lost in thought when I feel someone touch my leg under the water. I stop swimming and float, looking around me. The boys are still on the side of the pool talking and Trixie pops up beside me.

"Dad just shouted over the fence that the pizza has just arrived."

We both climb out, grabbing our towels and go back to her house. After we both change into our pyjamas, we sit in the living room with our pizza. Trixie puts a DVD on, Mamma Mia.

"I'm going to head to bed, you girls don't stay up to late okay?" Steve says.

We both agree and turn back to the film.

Twenty minutes into the movie, Zeke appears.

"Hey Zork, where are mum and dad?

Trixie points to the ceiling and ignores him.

"What's her deal, why is she in a mood?" he asks me.

I open my mouth to reply, but Trixie beats me to it.

"She has a name and is trying to watch a film, so bugger off with your friends and leave us alone."

I glance at Zeke and shrug.

"Fine moody mare, I'm getting my pizza and going back next door. I'm staying over there tonight. Good luck JC with her, she's a right stroppy cow today." he says, then leaves us, grabbing his pizza on the way out.

"Jackass." Trixie says and I gaze at her. She doesn't say anymore and we go back to the film.

Forty minutes later I glance over and she's out cold on the sofa, sleeping. I grab the black throw from the back of it and place it over her. I take our dishes into the kitchen to wash them, before grabbing my book from upstairs. I step out on to the patio, sit on the sun lounger and start reading. A strange feeling comes over me, like I was being watched. I glance up and look around the back garden, but don't see anyone. I look at the fence that divides Aunt Lucy's and Colby's house, and notice that Colby is leaning on the fence staring me

"Jesus, you scared me. You know it's creepy to just stand and stare at someone in the shadows, right?" I say, he jumps over the fence and stalks towards me.

I close my book and sit up straighter, lifting my legs as he sits on the edge of the sun lounger and places them over his lap. My heart starts racing again from the heat of his touch. My hands begin to tremble, so I place them under my thighs.

"So, today was fun," he smiles while rubbing my leg.

"Yeah it was, thanks for teaching me."

"So, what does JC stand for?"

I smile at him as he's sweet. "JC is short for Jodi Collins, but everyone calls me JC."

"Jodie, that's a cute name, why don't you go by that instead of JC?"

"It's what my dad uses to call me and it's stuck ever since."

He stops rubbing my leg, then looks me in the eyes.

"I'm sorry JC, tell me about your dad, what was he like?"

Moving my hands from under my thighs I place them on my lap, twisting them together.

"My dad was my hero; he would do anything for me. One day he was driving home from work and he was hit by a lorry, killed instantly."

I feel the tears starting to fall, Colby moves my legs off his lap and pulls me closer to him, wrapping his one arm around my shoulder.

"JC, I'm sorry I shouldn't have brought it up..."

"Colby, it's fine, I like talking about him. It's just hard with him not being here. I know Aunt Lucy and mum found it difficult when he died. My best friend Josie, is the only person that knows what I went through. She stayed by my side even after I was a right cow towards her."

"JC..." Colby starts to say when my phone starts ringing. Taking it out of my pocket I glance down, its Josie, video messaging me on Facebook.

"I'll leave you to answer your friend..."

"Please stay?" I beg, he agrees and I swipe across the screen to answer the call, Josie appears on the phone.

"JC, Oh my god I miss you. I wish you would come home early; Craig is…" she pauses when she notices Colby. "Hey hot stuff what's your name?"

Colby laughs, "Hey, I'm Colby, I live next door to JC's cousins."

"JC, you've been holding out on me, with Mr Muscle sat next to you, living next door. Are you sleeping together?" she asks bluntly.

"Josie." I yell a little louder than I should have.

"What? I'm your best friend, I am allowed to ask…"

"Josie, don't be rude. Just because you are my best friend, doesn't give you a right to ask questions like that, with Colby sat right here. Be nice." I tell her and she makes a funny face and rolls her eyes.

"Okay sorry. Well Craig has been asking about you, he can't wait for you to come home. Oh, I almost forgot, the house opposite yours is empty. So, you will have new neighbours by the time you come home."

Colby links his hand through my free one. I glance sideways at him and he winks.

"Hey lovebirds, I'm still here you know."

I smile at her, "How has your summer been so far?"

"It's been okay, not the same without you. Symon asked me to go to a party with him. I'll tell you more about him next time. I've been hanging out with Symon and Craig a lot, a group of us are going camping over the weekend."

"Sounds like you're having a good one so far…"

"Oh shoot, I need to go, Symon just text. I'll text you later," she says, then she was gone.

"Sorry about Josie, she tends to jump to the wrong conclusion all the time." I explain to Colby.

"Can I seen your phone a second?" he asks and I pass it over to him. He types in his number and lets his phone ring once in his pocket. "There, now you have my number."

I stand up, "Sit on the sun lounger and take some photos so I can remember this night by" I say.

He sits back on the sun lounger and I sit between his legs before I open the camera app on my phone.

"Let's take some selfies." I say and we snap a few with my camera, before switching to my Snapchat app and take a few more with filters.

"Hey Colby, how about you get your arms off my cousin and get back over to your own house?"

We both look up and Zeke is leaning on the fence.

"How long have you been standing there standing like a creeper?" Colby asks.

"Long enough to know JC's best friend thinks you are hooking up, when she saw you."

I jump up, "Zeke, nothing is going on with me and Colby, we're just friends. Josie is always jumping to the wrong conclusion; we were just talking." I explain.

Colby stands and walks over to Zeke.

"Z, you're not her father, so mind your own business. Like Jodi just said we were just talking. I'm not going to be rude and ignore her." Colby tells him before jumping over the wall. "Night Jodi", he says with his back to Zeke and winks, then walks inside his house with Zeke.

I feel like a puddle of goo, he called me by my first name not once but twice and it felt good. I smile then grab my book and head inside to bed.

Chapter Six

Pool Party

The first week and half at Aunt Lucy's, flies by. I've been spending most of the time at the beach, with Zeke, Colby, and Trixie. The boys spend a lot of time surfing. They have been trying to teach me to balance on the board on my own and get comfortable being on the it, before trying to surf on my own.

Colby texts me at night, and we spend ages messaging back and forth. He asks me about my life back home and my friends, he tells me about his brother and the competitions he's won. About how he wants to do an event that's coming up. We have become good friends since we started hanging out, sometimes he flirts, giving me butterflies.

After the last time I FaceTime with Josie, I have spoken to her on another two occasions. She always asks how Mr Muscles aka Colby is.

Today is Friday and Ross is having a pool party next door; the music is blasting. Colby invites us over to join in the party. I walk over with Trixie, as Zeke was already there. As we enter the back garden, there are people everywhere. I spot Nicole sitting across from the pool with a few other girls talking. I stop and face Trixie.

"Trix, are you sure you want to be here? I know you hate Nicole …" I say in a low voice, but she cuts me off.

"I'm fine JC, I will just ignore her." she replies before dumping her bag by the fence. She then walks over to the pool and jumps in like a cannonball. I place my bag beside hers and walk over to the edge and look for Zeke. He's in the corner kissing a girl with red hair. I feel weird walking up and interrupting them, so I go and see if I can find Colby.

He is sat on a blanket on the grass, drinking a can of coke, with two girls sat either side of him in swimsuits. I change my mind, turn around and smack straight into Ross.

"Hey there speedy, where's the fire? Where are you off to in such a rush?" he asks.

I tense up like I been caught with my hand in the cookie jar.

"I umm. I need the toilet; do you know where it is?" I ask. He just laughs. "Omg can't believe I asked you that. Of course, you know it's …"

Ross cuts me off, "JC, chill upstairs, first door on the right."

I head into the house, closing the patio door behind me. I walk up the stairs, pausing along the way to look at all photos that are hanging on the wall. Colby and Ross were cute kids growing up and now they are both still yummy to look at.

After five minutes of looking at all the photos, I find the toilet, I walk in, closing and locking the door behind me. After I'm done, I wash and dry my hands then unlock the door. As I open it, Colby is stood there, leaning against the door frame.

"Sorry, I just washed my hands. were you waiting to use the toilet?" I ask. He shakes his head.

"No, Ross said you came up to use the bathroom, so I wanted to see if you were okay."

I walk towards him and stand in front of him.

"I'm fine. You shouldn't worry about me."

Colby reaches out, grabbing my hand, then pulls me into the room next to the bathroom and closes the door.

"JC, I wanted…" He doesn't have the chance to finish as the door opens.

"Colby, there you are, why you up here, the party is downstairs?" Ross says as he glances between us.

"I wanted to talk to JC…"

"Dude, talk later, party now." He says, then grabs his arm, pulling him down the stairs. I follow them down and go in search of Trixie. When I find her, she is sitting on the side of the pool with two other girls.

"Hey JC, this is Kim," she points to the one girl, "This is Jaz" she says pointing to the other girl. "Girls this is JC, my cousin" she adds.

I give them a small wave.

"Hey girls". I smile and they both wave back. I sit down and join them, listening to them talk about their last few months in school. Zoning out, I gaze across the pool, and I notice Colby and Ross having a heated conversation with an older woman I recognise from the photos from earlier. It looks like she's their mother. Ross is pointing his finger angrily at her, while Colby grips his hair like he's about to explode. Trixie waves her hand in front of my face to get my attention.

"You zoned out on us. You okay?' She asks and glances in the direction that I was looking. "Oh, that can't be good." She whispers. I whip my head to look at her.

"Why is that?"

"Ross never gets angry or talks to his mum the way he is now. Zeke?" She calls to her brother, motioning for him to come over. He swims over to us.

"What's up Dork?" he asks and she points to where Ross and Colby are with their mother.

"Flaming hell," he curses, then jumps out the pool and walks over to them.

A few seconds later, Mrs Ryan walks off inside and Colby storms off out the side gate, where Zeke chases after him. I stand up from the pool and go get my bag to check my phone. I notice that I have a missed call from Josie, I swipe across to get rid of the notification and send a text to Colby.

Me: Are you okay?

There is no reply, so I put my phone back in my bag and put it back by Trixie's.

Two hours pass by and I still haven't heard from Colby or Zeke. Ross is sitting on the side of the pool beside Trixie and me. Trix is hanging on his every word. He hasn't mentioned what's going on with his mother, so I ask

"Hey Ross, do you know where Colby is?"

He shakes his head

"No, no idea" he replies and goes back to talking to Trixie.

Lifting my legs out of the pool, I stand up and grab the towel off the chair, wrapping it around my waist.

"Trix, have you had any text messages or miss calls from Zeke or Colby.?" I ask, she shakes her head.

"JC, I'm sure they are fine, you know…"

Before she can say anymore, she is interrupted by Nicole.

"Aww does little JC have a crush on Colby? Think you need to cool off." She says, before pushing me into the pool, making me bang my head on the side of it. Everything goes black.

Everything around me sounds so quiet.

"What happened?" a male voice says.

"That bitch pushed her in the pool and she banged her head." A female voice responds.

"Why did you push her Nic? She's done nothing wrong to you. You better damn well hope she wakes up or so help me god." Another male voice says.

I feel that someone is rubbing my hand.

"Sweetheart can you hear me?" a soft voice says.

I slowly open my eyes. Aunt Lucy is holding my one hand with teary eyes, standing behind her is Uncle Steve. Trixie and Zeke are kneeling on the other side.

"Oh my god, JC you scared us. How are you feeling sweetie?" Aunt Lucy asks.

"I'm ok my head hurts," I say touching my head and notice blood on my fingers.

"Okay everyone, move back, let's get JC to the hospital to get checked out." Uncle Steve says.

"I'm fine, can I just go home and go to bed?" I try to argue but Aunt Lucy cuts in.

"JC, Steve is right you need to go to the hospital to be on the safe side"

They both help me up, but I feel shaky on my legs.

"Here sit her on the chair. She doesn't look too clever on her feet." Ross says placing a chair behind me to sit on. I sit down for a moment. My head is banging feels like I've been kicked in the head.

"Aunt Lucy, I can't walk, I don't feel steady on my feet" I say. I glance up and see Colby out of the corner of my eye walking through the side gate. He notices everyone stood by me and walks toward me, then he sees the blood on my head.

"Jesus JC, what happened, are you okay?" he asks crouching down to check me all over.

"Dumbo pushed her in the pool and she hit her head on the side of the pool." Trixie spits, whilst pointing over at Nicole. Colby's head shoots in her direction

"What Nicole did this? I'm going to kick her ass…." before he can continue, Ross butts in.

"Colby, not now. JC needs to be checked out. Go get her something to put over her swimming costume," he orders.

Colby stands up, runs in the house and rushes upstairs to get some clothes. Uncle Steve and Ross carry me into the house and place me on the sofa.

Five minutes later Colby is back with some clothes.

"Okay boys out," Aunt Lucy orders and she helps me put on the shorts and T shirt Colby brought down. Once I'm dressed, Uncle Steve and Aunt Lucy take me to A & E to be checked out.

Chapter Seven

The BBQ

After the accident at the pool party, I was kept in the hospital for a few days as a precautionary measure. When they finally discharged me, Aunt Lucy wouldn't stop fussing and Trixie has been like my shadow.

I've been back at Aunt Lucy's for a few days since coming out of hospital. I haven't left my room much, as I've been resting and catching up on my reading. I've text Colby a few times, but he's not replying. I don't know why, but I am worried about him.

There is a knock on the door and Trixie pokes her head in.

"JC mums made some pasta for dinner," she says then motions to follow her downstairs.

We all sit around the table, but Zeke is missing. He walks in just as we start eating with Colby and Ross.

"What have you boys been up to?" Uncle Steve asks.

"Just sorting some stuff out." Colby replies, before Ross cuts in.

"Mr and Mrs Matthews, my mother is having a BBQ later and she has some news she wants to share. Will you call come?"

"Sounds good. What time do you want us, do you need us to bring anything? Aunt Lucy asks before going back to her meal.

"No, we have everything covered, any time after six will be fine." He says then he pushes Colby to go and he follows behind. Zeke sits down at the table, after grabbing his food Aunt Lucy had left in the microwave for him. He starts shovelling the pasta in his mouth with his fork, like he is dying of starvation.

"Z, do you know what is going on with the Ryan boys? They were arguing with their mother at the pool party," Trix asks.

"Yeah Colby told me but it's not for me to say," he explains.

"Trixie, leave it be. Whatever is going on we will find out later, now finish your food." Uncle Steve tells her.

Once we have finished our meal, myself and Trixie wash up and head upstairs to my room. I sit on the bed and lean against the wall, while Trixie lays down on with her feet dangling off the end.

"Was it just me or did Colby looked uncomfortable being in the same room as me, or is it just my imagination?" I ask.

Trix props herself up on to her side and glances up at me.

"JC, I don't know what is going on with Colby, I wouldn't take it personally. I just think they have something going on. I know the boys shut themselves off the last time when something serious happened before." She explains just as my phone rings. I turn is over and check who it is, it's Josie. Swiping across the screen I answer.

"Hey Josie, what's up?"

She has a beaming smile on her face.

"JC, oh my god I miss you…" She pauses glancing to the side then bites her lip. "JC are you alone." She asks, acting a bit weird.

"No Trix is here, what's going on, why you being strange?" I ask.

"Okay I have someone here that wants to talk to you" she says before the screen goes blurry and then Craig appears. I glance at Trixie and she motions she's leaving to give me privacy I move from sitting up to laying on my stomach.

"Hi Craig." I say nervously and he smirks.

"Hey JC, how is your summer going?"

"It has been really good so far, had accident a few days ago. I hit my head on the side of the pool and ended up in A & E, but I am fine now. I'm going to a BBQ later, what about you?"

"It's been pretty boring here, gone to a few parties, but it would be better when you come back." he says then winks.

He's flirting with me like he did back at Symon's house.

"Maybe when you come back, I can take you out on a date?"

I can feel the heat rising, I've had a crush on Craig for ages but something has changed this summer.

"Yeah maybe we can all go out, all four of us," I offer.

"Yeah that be cool. Can't wait for you to come back, Josie is pining for you as well," he says and the phone is snatch from him and Josie is back.

"Ignore that idiot I am not pining for you, "she laughs. "I do miss you though, are you sure you can't come home earlier than you said?" she asks and I shake my head

"I can't it's only been two weeks; I still have another two left. Josie has Craig left the room? "I ask and she nods.

"Why, what's wrong?" she asks.

"Remember when you Face Timed me and I had the boy next door with me?" she nods so I continue. "Well he has me feeling things for him. We kind of had a moment at his pool party the other day, like he was going to kiss me but we were interrupted. He's been acting weird since. I'm not sure what to do." I explain and turn over onto my back.

"Wow JC, that's crazy. Do you like him more than Craig?"

"Yeah, I do, which is weird because I have only known him a short time," I reply and Josie's eyes nearly pop out of her head.

"Oh my god JC. This is big what are you going to do?"

"I don't know, that's why I am talking to my best friend, asking for advice." I reply sarcastically.

"Okay, so I know what you need to do. Find the cutest outfit and when you go to the BBQ corner him and tell him how you feel. Be honest, most boys like that and if he acts like a tool, make your excuses, and leave early. Then you can come home and hook up with Craig."

I cut her off, "Really Josie? I will not hook up with another guy on a rebound." I shout.

"Jesus JC, take a chill pill will you. Fine don't hook up with Craig, just go out on one date with him to keep him happy."

"Okay maybe I better go I have stuff to sort out before I go to the BBQ in a few hours," I say then end the call.

A few hours later I am dressed in blue denim shorts, a white tank top and sandals and heading over to the Ryan's next door with my Aunt, Uncle, Trixie, and Zeke. When we arrive, Mrs Ryan is standing by the big black, metal BBQ in the corner of the garden, flipping burgers and turning chicken drumsticks with a glass of wine in her other hand. There is a big garden table with eight chairs around it and an umbrella in the centre. A few bowls of salad, potatoes, bread, and pasta cover the table. Along with bottles of salad cream, Caesar salad dressing and mayonnaise. Aunt Lucy and Uncle Steve walk over and start talking to her, Zeke walks over to Ross and Colby.

Trixie grabs my hand and pulls me with her over to the chairs on the other side of the pool and sit down.

"Hey JC, are you okay?" she asks and we both glance across the pool to where the boys are sitting. Colby is staring at us; he's making me feel super nervous.

"Foods nearly ready, if you want to grab a drink then we can all sit at the table" Mrs Ryan says.

We grab drinks and go over to the table; Aunt Lucy and Mrs Ryan are lost in conversation as the boys join us. Colby sits on the chair next to me, my heart is racing so fast it feels like it's going to jump out. Mrs Ryan places the food from the BBQ on the serving platters, and we all help ourselves. The boys are talking about surfing. Mrs Ryan, Aunt Lucy, and Uncle Steve are in a full-blown conversation the other side. Trixie is texting on her phone, sat next to me. I can't take it any longer I feel like I am about to burst.

"Mrs Ryan, is it okay if I can use the toilet?" I ask interrupting their conversation.

"Sure sweetie, you remember where it is from the other day?" she asks and I nod and get up from the table taking my phone with me and go to the toilet. Closing the door, as I take care of business my phone buzzes. Its Colby.

JC, I am sorry I haven't been replying to your messages. There is a lot going on, from the first day I set my eyes on you I fancied you like crazy.

I'm in shock, but I reply.

Colby, I don't know what to say. You have me lost for words.

JC, I have been acting like a fool. I was hoping to have the whole summer with you, but I won't now.

He's being weird again, why won't we have the whole summer I wonder. I was about to reply, when there's a knock on the door.

"Hey sweetie, are you okay? We were just a little worried you were taking ages." My Aunt says.

I pull my shorts up, flush the toilet then wash my hands. Putting my phone in my pocket, I open the door.

"I'm fine," I tell her and we go back down stairs to join the others. Colby's seat is empty, he's standing by his mother with Ross. he has annoyed look on his face. Once myself and Aunt Lucy are sitting down, Mrs Ryan places the glass she was holding on the table.

"Well I didn't think this would be so hard to say." she says pausing.

"Chloe it can't be that bad. What's the news?" Aunt Lucy asks.

"Okay, well I have known you for over fourteen years so I wanted you to be the first to know after my boys." she smiles squeezing Ross and Colby's shoulders. "I have accepted a new job and we will be moving next week. I know it's kind of fast, but I have found a new house. For the time being I will be renting this house out," she says smiling.

Colby pushes his mother's arm off his shoulder and storms inside and Ross chases after him.

"Oh, my word, that's amazing Chloe. We're sure are going to miss you, how are the boys taking the move?" she asks.

Mrs Ryan sighs, "Ross is okay, but Colby not so much."

Trixie nudges me, "I told you something wasn't right. Do you want to talk to him?" she asks and I nod.

"I think I should, I'd probably get through to him right now, better than Ross or his mother."

"Then go talk to him." Trix says, giving me a little push in the direction he went in. I quickly run through the back door, as I do, I hear Aunt Lucy ask Trix if I'm okay, but I don't hear her reply. I pause at the bottom of the stairs when I see Ross coming down and he stops in front of me.

"JC, I don't think it's a good idea if you are going to see Colby right now. He's not in the right frame of mind..." He pauses, then he continues. "I shouldn't be telling you this, but you are the first girl that's got into his heart. Normally he likes the thrill of the chase when it comes to girls, but with you, you've got him in a right tail spin. I can see it when he looks at you. It's love in his eyes. I know he wanted to talk to you but then our mother dropped this bombshell on us. He thought he had a few more weeks with you, but we are. moving in a couple of days, that's why he's being the way he is. Look I have said more than I should have," he says then walks past. I continue up the stairs, and notice his Colby's bedroom door is wide open. He's sitting on the bed, leaning forwards with his hands in his hair. I walk in and stand in front of him then crouch down. "Colby, talk to me," I whisper and he drops his hands from his head and glances up at me.

"Colby, Ross said some stuff just now. Is it true?"

He shifts and sits up straight, "Ross has a big mouth… but it's true. They say that there is no such thing as love at first sight, but they are so wrong, because in a short space of time I am hundred percent crazy about you," he confesses.

I pull him up to a standing position, and wrap my arms around his body, holding him and he does the same.

"Forget about everything else, just hold me tight and live in the now." I say and he wraps his arms around me even tighter.

"I'll never forget you Jodi, the first girl to hold my heart."

"You are amazing guy Colby, after spending these last few weeks with you, I am crazy about you as well. Will you take me out on your board every day until you leave?"

"I'll do anything to spend time alone with you. I'm going to miss you when we have to leave."

I let go of him for a moment and cup his face with both hands.

"Just because our time is coming to an end, doesn't mean we won't talk or see each other. We will FaceTime every day, you won't get rid of me that easy." I tell him then wrap .my arms around his body again. The one thing that I have learnt is, if you want something then you have to fight for it.

Chapter Eight

Surfing Lessons

Waking up the next morning, I turn over and grab my phone. Swiping across the screen, I check my social media. A few photos pop up of Josie and Symon, as well as a few with Craig. They look like they have been having fun. My phone beeps with an incoming text message, its Colby.

Ready for a surfing lesson?

Sure, what time do you want to go? I'm still in bed, I haven't long woken up yet.

How about now, get dressed and leave a note for Lucy and Steve, telling them your with me.

What about breakfast? Shouldn't we eat first?

Have breakfast and then meet me at the bottom of the drive.

Okay see you in a bit.

Twenty minutes later, I've had breakfast. I'm dressed in my two-piece swimming costume and walking out of the house with my bag and towel. I can see Colby waiting for me, leaning against the garden wall with his surfboard beside him and a towel tossed over his shoulders.

"Morning sweetness," he says as I stop in front of him.

"Morning Colby. You're looking happy today." I say smiling. He reaches out grabbing my hand, pulling me towards him.

"I'm happy because I get to spend time alone with such a beautiful girl.' he says sweetly, then brings my right hand up to his mouth and kisses it.

"Should we get going?" I ask him and he nods in agreement. We walk to the beach slowly and he asks me about my friends back home. I tell him about Josie who he's already met when she FaceTime me. We talk about how our last year in high school went and he tells me about the school prom. He wasn't going to go but he ended up going with Trixie, as her boyfriend dumped her just before their prom. He is one of the nicest boys I have hung out with in a while.

We walk along the sand until we are in the middle of the beach, then Colby sticks his surfboard in the sand to stand it up. I lay my towel on the sand and drop my bag on top of it. Then kick of my flip flops placing them beside my bag and sit down. Colby follows, laying his towel beside nine and kicking his flip flops off before sitting on the towel beside me.

"So, is everything okay with you and your mother now?" I ask. He doesn't say anything, just stares out at the ocean. "Colby?" I say while placing my hand on the top of his leg.

He turns his head to look as me.

"JC, can we talk about something else, I don't want it to ruin my mood," he replies. "Let's go down to the sea while its quiet," he adds changing the subject.

"Sure," I say and stand up, taking my shorts and tank top off revealing my pink and black, two-piece swimsuit. He stands up, grabs the board and we walk down to the sea. Colby lays the surfboard on the water, gets on and paddles out. Before jumping up and standing on the board. He looks amazing when rides the waves, you can tell he's been doing it for a long time. As I watch him, the more mesmerised I become with the way he moves so easily against the waves. I slowly walk into the water as he comes down off of a wave and paddles towards me. Sitting up on his board, he runs his fingers through his hair, like something out of a shampoo advert. The water is really cold, but it doesn't bother me. I feel like I'm having an out of body experience, that's the effect Colby has on me.

"JC, are you n okay? You were staring off into space." He asks.

"I'm okay, just thinking about some stuff. You look amazing out there riding the waves, you should enter some surfing competitions." I say, changing the subject.

"Thanks, I've learnt from the best, my brother. Climb on, I'll take you out and we can ride a few low waves together." He says and helps me climb up on to his surfboard.

He paddles us out and we spend first hour riding low waves together. Colby then suggests I try it on my own.

"JC, you can do it, you're getting the hang of it now," he says before jumping off and leaving me on the board on my own.

"You can't be serious? What if I fall off…"

Cutting me off he says, "Jodi, trust me you will be fine. I promise I will not let anything happen to you. I'll be right here watching," he says then he pushes the surfboard forward.

I get a sudden burst of confidence and climb on to my stomach and start paddling forward. A wave comes towards me so I jump up and ride it. The rush I get from riding my first wave, ignites a fire inside me and I want more. Coming down from the wave, I float on the spot, it's then I notice a massive wave coming towards me. I start paddling hard and as fast as my arms let me. Just as I am about to bend my knees to stand, it knocks me off the board, sending me flying into the water.

The fantastic feeling of the rush, suddenly changes to one of panic. I start to flap my arms around, and I feel like the sea is going to swallow me and I'm going to drown. A set of arms grab me from under the water, pulling me out of the sea. It was Colby. I can't stop coughing; I swallowed some water while I was under.

"Jesus girl you scared the hell out of me, I thought..." he pauses. "Don't ever try and do that again JC. You haven't been surfing long enough to try a big wave like that. You are crazy," he says.

After about ten minutes pass by, I manage to stop coughing.

"I... it was a rush, the adrenalin kicked in. I rode the small wave and I needed more. Then I notice the big one and it was calling me..."

"Wow, you must have hit your head. Come on let's go up on the beach and chill before we go back for lunch."

He helps me up and grabs his surfboard from the water, then we walk up the beach, to where our towels are. He tosses his surfboard on the sand, then grabs his towel, giving it a little shake to get the sand off. He then wraps it around my shoulders.

"Colby, I have a towel, you need this..."

"I don't need it. You just fell of the surfboard and had a shock. It fine," he orders.

I frown at him then sit down.

"Damn you're bossy. Come sit here," I say tapping the space beside me. He walks over and sits beside me, I grab my shorts, tank top, and make some sort of a pillow with them. I lay down, pulling Colby backwards with me, then I throw the towel over our arms.

"Thank you for saving me, you're my hero." I say. and turn to look at him.

He smiles and lifts his arm wrapping it around my shoulders pulling me close. I lay my head on his bare chest resting my hand on his stomach.

"Jodi you don't have to thank me, I'd do anything for you." He says, then kisses my head tenderly.

Closing my eyes and I relax on Colby's chest, listening to the sounds of the waves as they crash against the shore and the seagulls squawking above.

I must have fallen asleep as the next thing I feel is someone shaking me.

"Well this looks cosy, something you want to share?" Trixie teases. I glance up at her then at Colby, who is watching me like I'm some precious doll.

"Hey sleeping beauty, you've been sleeping for ages."

"It's nearly dinner time, mum sent me to come find you guys... but I think you are in good hands" Trixie says.

I untangle myself from Colby and quickly put my shorts and tank top back on.

"You girls go ahead I'm going to grab a few more waves before I head home," he says before cupping both sides of my face and kisses me on the forehead.

Grabbing his towel and surfboard, he walks towards the sea. Picking up my towel from the sand, I give it a shake to get the sand off. Throwing it over my shoulder, I stick my feet in my flip flops and grab my bag, as I look at Trixie, I notice she's watching me with a massive smile.

"What is tickling you? "I say. She's being weird just staring with a smile like that on her face, she reminds me of the Joker from Batman.

"You not going to say anything about what Colby just did? He just kissed you on the head."

I roll my eyes at her.

"There is nothing to say, he was just being nice." I reply and start walking ahead where Trixie has to run to catch up with me.

"Yeah being nice my ass, you have a crush on him and he has the hot's for you. I could see it a mile off. The way he touches you and the way you are when you are together. I think it's kind of sweet. I don't think I have ever seen him head over heels in love before, even Z has noticed a change in Colby since you came to stay."

"Okay fine, he did tell me he's crazy about me. I know this might sound insane, but I think I have fallen for him. He's sweet, caring, attentive, tender, lovely to talk to and hasn't once tried to kiss me on the lips. My heart races when he's near or touches me. My body comes alive; the fire inside ignites he…."

Trixie cuts me off. "Omg you love him, that dreamy look in your eyes, the way you gush about him, it's so obvious. Have you told him yet?"

I shake my head, "What's the point, I am only here for another week and half and he's leaving in the next few days."

"Aww JC, I wish you could have more time with him. You would make a cute couple." She says stopping, then hugging me. "Come on let's get back and have lunch. before mum sends a search party looking for us." She jokes.

Chapter Nine

Sunsets and Sweet Goodbyes

It's been a few hours since I last spoke to Colby. We had lunch, then I took a nap as all the surfing took it out of me. Despite falling asleep on Colby at the beach, I felt like I could sleep for a week.

My phone ringing wakes me from my sleep.

"Hello" I say sleepily, not bothering to see who it is.

"Hey sleepy head. Fancy coming over to mine to hangout?"

It's Colby. Holding my phone from my ear I check the time; it's coming up to half five.

"Wow, I guess I was more tired than I thought, I can't believe I've slept for this long. Sure I'll be over in twenty, I need to wake myself up a bit first. Do you want me to ask Zeke and Trixie?"

"Zeke and Ross went out about an hour ago and Trix followed, they have gone down to the beach. They won't be back for ages

"Okay, I'll see you in a bit "I tell him and then end the call.

I sit up and rub my eyes, before going to the bathroom to have a wash. I change into my white shorts and black tank top, then grab my bag and phone, before heading downstairs. Uncle Steve is on the sofa watching TV.

"How are you doing sleepyhead? Colby popped by earlier to see you, but you were out cold. He said you had fun surfing this morning and you came off the surfboard. Did you hurt yourself when you fell off?" he asks.

I shake my head, "No I didn't hurt myself; Colby came to my rescue." I say and smile.

Aunt Lucy walks into the room, "Hey sweetie, how are you?"

"I'm good, is it okay if I go next door to hangout?" I ask.

She smiles and her and Uncle Steve share a look.

"Sure, go ahead sweetie have fun.

"Aww I think our little JC has a crush," Uncle Steve adds.

I feel the heat rising in my cheeks.

"Leave her alone Steve. It's cute she has a crush, he's a nice boy." She tells him. "You go ahead JC, ignore him." She then playfully hits him on the back if the head.

I leave them to it and walk next door, the gate on the site squeaks as I push it open and close it behind me. Colby appears in front of me in blue shorts and a white t shirt.

"Hey beautiful," he smiles. "I heard the gate," he says answering the question that was on the tip of my tongue. We walk inside his house and he takes me upstairs to his bedroom.

All his stuff is packed up in boxes, black bags are in a pile by the wall. All the dark blue walls are bare..

"Wow, you packed up your room quick, last time I was in here you had no boxes packed up."

He glances at me, "Yeah I was in a right mood the other night, I stayed up until three in the morning packing my room up. Only thing left is to disconnect my TV and Xbox, then shove my bedding into a black bag."

I drop my bag on the floor in front of by his TV.

"Hey," I say walking up to him, grabbing his hands, linking mine in his. "Colby, you know this summer isn't over just yet, we still have a few days." I say as his facial expression changes.

"Actually, we don't, it's why I wanted to spend time with you this morning. Mum has a removal firm coming in the morning."

"Wow, she doesn't waste any time."

Colby leans forward, gently kissing me on the head.

"I know, I was really annoyed that's why I wanted to stay after Trix found us, so I don't have to speak to her. She makes me so angry that she doesn't think about anyone else apart from herself. I don't want to move; my friends are here and…"

Colby pauses, then pulls me towards him, wrapping his arms around me, "I wish we could have had more time together, she ruins everything," he says while holding me in his arms. I lay my head on his chest and hug him back. We stay like that for a short while.

"Come on, let's go down, grab some drinks and sit by the pool for a bit," he says while dropping his arms.

Making our way down the stairs, we grab a couple of bottles of water from the fridge in the kitchen, before going out to the pool, and sit on the sun loungers. Taking my phone out of my shorts, back pocket, I place it beside me on the table with our drinks.

"Colby you know you moving doesn't have to be the end, we can still be friends and talk everyday if you want. Maybe even FaceTime each other."

"I'd really like that and I could come visit you when we are settled into the new house. That's if your boyfriend wouldn't mind?" he says.

I smile at him. "I don't have a boyfriend back home, but if I did, he probably wouldn't be happy I'm hanging out with you over the summer." I joke.

Colby laughs while sitting up on the sun lounger and moves his legs so they are dangling over the sides, then pats the space in front of him.

"Come sit by me and take some photos so we can remember this summer."

Grabbing my phone, I sit in front of him, swipe across the screen and pull up my camera. I snap a few pictures. Colby then takes my phone, goes to my snapchat app and takes a few photos with various filters.

"Hey Colby, can I use the bathroom?" I ask him and he tells me to go ahead.

Ten minutes later and I'm back downstairs, I walk out the back and Colby is holding my bag.

"Everything okay?" I ask, feeling confused.

Is he kicking me out?

"Hey Jodi take that frown off your face. If tonight is our last night together alone, then I want to show you something amazing. Come on, it's not far," he says, being all mysterious.

"Okay." I say and take my bag from him.

"I put your phone and the water bottles in your bag. Let's go, we don't have long before the sun goes down," he says then takes my hand, leading me out of his back garden.

As we walk, he holds my hand the whole time, as he leads me down towards the beach. Just as I think he's taking me on there, we walk past, up a hill that overlooks the whole of the beach and the sea.

"This is one of my favourite places to come whenever I need to think. You can see for miles on a good day, you might even see the passing ferry. At night when the skies are clear, you can see all the stars including Orion's Belt from up here."

"Wow, why did you bring me up here? Not planning on pushing me over the edge, are you?" I joke.

He smirks, "No, I want to show you something. Come and sit with me here," he says holding out his hand.

I drop my bag on the grass, take his hand and we both sit down.

"I wanted to watch one last sunset before we move and I wanted to share it with the most beautiful girl in the world, you JC."

"Colby, you are so sweet, there is no other boy like you."

I lean across and kiss him on the cheek. "You truly are one of a kind Colby, more boys should be like you." I confess.

"Oh, really and what is it I am?" he flirtingly asks.

"You really want me to say it don't you?" I ask and he nods. "Fine, I will say it, you're charming, so caring and you wear your heart on your sleeve. You always think about your friends and your brother. You're the perfect guy; any girl would be lucky to have you as her boyfriend." I say, *I know I would.*

"Thanks JC, but the girl I want is… never mind, let's sit and watch the sunset." He says.

We sit there for thirty minutes, watching the sun go down over the ocean. The flecks of orange, red and yellow colour the sky as the sun drops down below the sea.

"Wow, that's one of the most beautiful things I have ever seen." I whisper as he glances at me.

"I would have to disagree; you are the most beautiful thing I have ever seen."

I turn from the sunset to face Colby, "You are so sweet, my heart melts when you say things like that. I wish things were different…"

He cuts me off by placing his finger over my mouth to silence me.

"Please don't say anything, I want to remember this moment, our sweet goodbye."

So, we sit there for another hour, before we walk back in the darkness to Aunt Lucy's. Tomorrow is going to be hard to watch him go. To have found the one you love, but not be able tell him you love him, it's going to be heartbreaking.

Chapter Ten

Regrets

My dreams were filled with Colby, his gorgeous face, his sweet smile. The way he tenderly kisses me on the forehead or on the nose, like I am some princess. I toss and turn all night, long the conversations we've had in the last few days, play over in my head. I know he wants to say something, but he is just holding it back, why? What is he scared to tell me?

It was gone two in the morning when I finally manage to fall asleep.

The sound of a truck door slamming, wakes me up. Glancing at the clock on my phone, I notice its nearly nine-thirty. Throwing the duvet cover back, I jump out of bed. Opening the bedroom door, I rush down the stairs and out the front door, rushing to next door. Mrs Ryan is standing there, "JC, what are you doing here? The removal men are here loading our stuff on to the van."

"Are the boys still here?" I ask. She shakes her head

"No sweetheart, Ross and Colby went with the first van load to the new house. We been up since six this morning." she explains.

"Oh." I say and start walking back to Aunt Lucy's.

"JC here, Colby said to give you this," she says holding out a letter. "He wants you to have his surfboard, I gave it to Zeke earlier, when he was over saying goodbye to the boys."

"Okay thanks, Mrs Ryan. " I say and head back over to Aunt Lucy's.

As I walk through the door, my aunt is stood at the bottom of the stairs.

"Come here sweetie." she says holding her arms out in a motherly way. I go to her and cry. "JC, are you okay honey? I know you were falling for him; we could all see it the way you looked at him and I think he felt the same about you."

My heart is hurting, it feels like its shattered into a thousand pieces

"Aunt Lucy, I wasn't just falling for him. I fell in love with him." I confess before breaking down in tears.

After half hour, I manage to stop crying and Aunt Lucy told me to go have a shower, while she made pancakes for breakfast. She had planned a girly day us and Trixie, to distract me. I guess I'd been so caught up, thinking about Colby all the time, that I hadn't done anything else.

My aunt had kicked Uncle Steve and Zeke out, and sent them to go do whatever father and sons do together. Trixie and her painted my nails, then we all put on mud masks to cleanse our skins, while we watched cheesy romcom films.

It was nice just relaxing, after we took our mud masks off, Aunt Lucy went into the cupboard under the stairs, pulling out a small shoe box.

"Mum what's in the box?" Trixie asks.

I'm handed the box, where my Aunt says, "This is a box of stuff that belonged to your dad. I think he would want you to have it."

I glance from her to the box. "Aunt Lucy do you mind if I go upstairs and look through it?"

She shakes her head and smiles, "You go on sweetie, if you have any questions, I'll be down here."

Taking the box upstairs, I place it on the bed and close the door. Sitting on the bed, I opened it. Inside there is a few photos and a letter. I look through the photos, there is one of dad with mum when they were younger. Also, there is one of my dad holding me when I was a baby and a photo of my dad, mum, and me with a Christmas tree in the background. Placing the photos back in the box, I pick up the white envelope, open it and begin reading.

> *To my darling baby girl,*
>
> *If you are reading this then your Aunt Lucy kept her promise. I wanted you to know how proud I am of you; I will be looking down from above keeping an eye on you. You will always be my little princess.*
>
> *I hope when the time comes you find a boy that is worthy to have you in his life, that he treats you like the princess you are.*
>
> *Always listen to your heart, fight for what you want and follow your dreams.*
>
> *Dream big princess, you can do anything you put your mind to.*
>
> *I wish I could be there for the important milestones; just remember baby girl everything happens for a reason.*
> *If something is meant to be, it will be.*
>
> *Love you always*
>
> *Dad*
> *XX*

The tears fall down my cheeks, hearing my dad's words make me feel like I am breaking inside. The last thing he said to me was that he would see me after school. Only he didn't, he was killed instantly when a lorry crashed into him, after the driver fell asleep at the wheel.

I'm knocked out of my memories when there is a knock on my door, and Aunt Lucy poked her head in.

"Oh sweetie," she says, then walks in wrapping her arms around me. "JC, I knew this was going to be hard for you. It's why I wasn't sure if I should have given you this box."

I wipe the tears away, place the letter and photos in my bag.

"I'm glad you did; some days are harder than most. Hearing him say he's proud of me, calling me his little princess makes me happy. I do miss him like crazy, but this letter has helped."

My phone chooses that moment to start ringing, I check the caller ID, its Josie Face Timing.

"I'll leave you to it, talk to your friend," Aunt Lucy says before walking out closing the door behind her.

"Hey Josie." I answer swiping the screen. Her face goes from happy and excited to worried when she sees me.

"JC, what's wrong, don't lie, tell me the truth?" she orders.

I make myself comfy on the bed, grabbing the photos and letter from my bag. I tell her about the box my Aunt gave me.

"Wow, that's a lot to take in. How are you feeling about it?"

"I guess I'm okay you know, I miss him but I'm glad I got to read the letter. I'm just…"

Josie cuts me off, "JC, I know you, there is more going on than you are letting on, what is it

I can't get anything past her, she can read me like a book.

"Colby is gone, his mother got a new job, I didn't even get to tell him goodbye or…." I pause trying to stop the tears from falling again.

"Tell him goodbye or what?" Josie asks.

"I… I can't."

"Oh JC, you love him. Aww babe it's written all over your face, you're head over heels in love."

I can't take it; I break down in tears.

"I feel so broken, first Colby, then the letter from my dad. I went over this morning, but I was too late. He had gone with the first truck load, with his brother to their new home. He left me a letter and he give me his surfboard."

"Aww JC, I'm so sorry. What did the letter say?"

"I haven't read it, after I came back to the house, I broke down and have been a mess since. Aunt Lucy and Trixie have been distracting me with girly stuff, so I haven't had a chance to read it yet."

"You should go read his letter and then call or text him."

I sigh, "I will, I don't want to be here anymore, Josie I want to come home. Summer is over."

Movement from the door catches my eye, its Zeke.

"Josie, I need to go, thanks for being there for me."

"That's what best friends are for JC, text me later," she says then hangs up.

I place my phone on the bed beside me.

"How long have you been standing by the door eavesdropping?" I ask him.

"Long enough to know you are in love with Colby. You know I've known him since we were small, both him and

Ross." He walks in and sits on the end of bed, "I think we all kind of guessed you liked each other. From that first day you arrived for the summer, he's been acting differently and he wanted to know everything about you. I think the final realisation of how he felt was when he took you on the surfboard the first time."

"I don't know what to say, I didn't get to say a proper goodbye. My biggest regret is that I didn't get to tell him how I really feel."

Zeke shakes his head, "I swear you and Trix are as bad as each other…"

I cut him off. "What's that supposed to mean?"

"It means you two are as bad as each other. You and Colby have danced around each other most of the summer and now he's gone. Trixie has been doing the same with Ross, only difference is he's completely blind. He can't see what is right in front of him. Trix thinks I haven't noticed, but I knew ages ago. Whenever he would have a girl around, Trixie would get annoyed and be all moody. Look if you really want to tell him, phone him, he deserves to know," he says then leaves my room.

After he's gone, I take out my Fallen Too Far book by Abbi Glines and start reading. Rush reminds me of Colby, both sweet and protective, with little coldness on the surface.

Chapter Eleven

Goodbye Summer

I've been completely lost in my book for a few hours, that I don't notice the sun had gone down. Trixie walks in my room,

"Hey book nerd," she jokes. "You had your head in that book for ages, mum has come up twice and you were still in the same spot. Put the book down and come have some food, its Pizza night."

I close the book and stand up, then we both head downstairs.

"There's my girls, are you hungry?" she asks as Zeke bounces down the stairs past us and sits at the table.

"I am sooo hungry, I could eat a horse." he says.

Uncle Steve hits him over the head, "You are always starving, I don't know where you put it all the food you eat." he says to him before sitting at the side of Zeke.

"I'm a growing boy, I need to eat."

"Yeah, eat me out of house and home." Aunt Lucy adds.

We all joined Uncle Steve and Zeke at the table.

"I am a little hungry," I say, while sitting opposite Zeke.

"Me too," Trixie adds, as she sits beside me.

Aunt Lucy takes a seat at the top of the table and we start eating.

"Oh, I almost forgot, I found this on the floor earlier by the sofa," she says holding out Colby's unopened letter.

"Thanks." I say taking it from her and placing it on the table beside my plate. We finish eating our pizza and then clear the table.

"Aunt Lucy is it okay if I go for a walk on my own?" I ask her.

"Sure sweetie, Zeke and Trixie can wash up," she replies.

I leave the table with the letter and go upstairs to change out of my pyjamas, that I had been in all day. Grabbing my denim blue shorts and white tank top from the wardrobe, I change into them and slip my flip flops on. Grabbing my bag, I toss the letter and my phone inside, and shove it up onto my shoulder. Before going downstairs and out the front door. I glance next door, half expecting to see Ross or Colby, but there is nothing. I walk down the street past the entrance to the beach where a few cars pass me by. I know where I want to go, it's the only place that Colby took me. The cliff overlooking the beach and ocean. As I walk up the grassy hill, I glance over at the beach, a few dog walkers are there with their dogs. Dropping my bag on the floor I sit on the grass; it feels weird being here without

Colby. Taking the letter from my bag, start reading before it gets dark.

> Jodi,
>
> I never knew what love was until I met you, the moment my eyes met yours, I was under your spell.
>
> When I close my eyes, all I see is you. I think about you from morning until night.
>
> You are the vision of beauty that plagues my dreams and the girl that got away.
>
> I will be miserable without you and will miss you terribly.
>
> If only fate hadn't took me away, I'd be still with you.
>
> We may be miles apart, but you will be the first girl to steal my heart.
>
> Love Colby

Folding the letter, I place it inside my bag then lie down, Colby's words have me crying again. Taking my phone out of my bag, I swipe across the screen until I find my photo gallery and open it. I scroll through all the photos, until I come to the photos of myself and Colby. He just stares back at me, with his gorgeous smile, jet-black hair, all messy. If only things were different, maybe we could have been more than friends. I was hoping to find a summer romance but what I happened was my heart was taken. This summer is well and truly over. I put my phone on the grass beside me and gaze up to the sky. All the stars are bright and clear. Orion's belt is directly above me, three stars in a row, close together.

Colby was right, the view from up on the cliff top is beautiful day and night. A shooting star crosses the sky, it's not something that is seen very often. Closing my eyes, I make a wish. When I open them a few minutes later, I just lay there, it's so peaceful. The only sounds you can hear are the waves as they crash against the shore, with the faint noise of cars passing, down by the main road.

My tears have dried up, but my mind is still on Colby, I hope he is okay in his new house. My phone starts ringing beside me, it's Aunt Lucy

"Hello." I answer.

"Hey sweetie, are you okay? You have been gone a few hours."

"I won't be long; I want to speak to you and Uncle Steve before I go bed."

"Okay sweetie, we will be waiting when you get home. Be safe," she says, then hangs up.

I stand up and take a few photos of the view with my phone, before walking back to the house.

As I walk through the front door Aunt Lucy and Uncle Steve look up from the sofa.

"Everything okay JC?" Uncle Steve asks.

I make my way over to the chair, after closing the front door and sit down, placing my bag on the floor.

"I wanted to say thank you for having me this summer, it's been amazing, spending time with you guys, Trixie and Zeke, but I miss my friends back home. I know I was meant to be staying another week, but I'd really like to go home on Friday."

"Oh, JC we have loved having you here, please tell me this is not because of Colby?" My aunt asks.

I want to tell her it's not, but the truth is, it is.

"No, I just miss my friends." I lie.

Aunt Lucy stands up, "Come here," she says holding her arms out. "JC, I am going to miss you when you go back home. We all will, but if you want to go home early then I will take you. Just remember you will always be welcome here anytime." she says hugging me tightly.

"Darling, I think your cutting of her air supply." Steve teases and she lets me go.

"Thanks again, I'll see you in the morning." I say, walking up the stairs. I enter my room and turn on the light, and I'm startled.

"Jesus Trixie, you scared me what are you doing sitting in in my room in the dark?" I say holding my hand to my chest.

"I can't believe you want to go home early; I'm going to miss you. It has been nice having another girl my age around the house."

Closing the door, I walk in and drop my bag on the floor, before sitting on the bed.

"I will miss you too Trix, maybe next time, you can stay with us." I suggest and she smiles.

"I'd love that. If you are leaving on Friday, can we have a movie night tonight?" she asks.

I nod my head. "Sure."

Friday is finally here and this summer break is finally over. As I load the last of my bags into the back of my Aunt's car, I quickly glance next door.

"Looks like you will have new neighbours," I say as Zeke walks down from the house with Colby's surfboard.

"Man, you are so Lucky JC, Colby giving you his surfboard. This was his baby, the first ever surfboard he ever had and now it's yours," he says as Steve takes it from him, tying it to the roof of the car.

"Call me okay. I want us to keep in touch." Zeke says and gives me a hug.

"Darling, drive carefully with the surfboard on the roof." My Uncle tells my Aunt before giving her a kiss. He then walks around the car to hug me.

"Okay girls let's get going, we don't want to get stuck in traffic." Lucy says and we all pile in the car.

Chapter Twelve

The Reunion

UB40 playing on the CD player fills the car as Aunt Lucy drives. We talk about summer and they both avoid talking about Colby. We stop off on the way to get drinks from McDonald's, Aunt Lucy went inside instead of the drive-through, as she was worried she may knock the surfboard off.

It doesn't take us long before we are back on the road.

"Mum have you told JC yet?" Trixie asks her mum.

"No, I was going to surprise her." she replies while looking in rear-view mirror. "Thanks for spoiling it."

"Sorry Mum," Trixie says.

"What surprise?" I ask.

"Well, rather than drive straight back, we are going to be staying with you until Sunday. I'm taking your Mum out for a girls night and you two get to hang out some more.

You can show Trixie your hometown while we are here." She says smiling.

"That would be amazing." I say just as my phone rings, its Josie.

"Hey JoJo," I say.

"You sound happier than when I last spoke to you, what's going on?"

"I'm coming home early; we are about another hour away..."

She squeals, so I pull the phone away from my ear and laugh.

"Oh my god JC, I so happy, I'll be waiting for you at your house," she says rather excitedly.

"Josie, Aunt Lucy and my cousin Trixie are staying the weekend, so you can meet them too."

"Josie I'm putting you on loudspeaker. Say hi to my aunt and cousin."

"Hey guys. JC, there is a UV Party tonight down the old community centre. It's going to be epic, please say we can all go?" She begs.

"You girls should go have fun." Aunt Lucy says.

"Okay fine we'll go, I have got to go I'll see you soon," I tell her before hanging up.

One thing I have learned over the years about Josie, is that when she's overly excited she rambles on about random stuff.

An hour later we are pulling up outside my house and before Aunt Lucy had even turned the car engine off, I am unbuckling my seat belt and swinging the door open. I jump out of the car and run over to my best friend, who is running down the path towards me.

"Oh my god, you're finally back." Josie says, squeezing me in a hug.

"I missed you too JoJo." I say hugging her back.

"I am so excited about tonight now you are back; this summer has been boring. Now that my partner in crime is here, it's going to be so much better." Josie says as Aunt Lucy and Trixie get out of the car.

"Josie, this is Aunt Lucy and my cousin Trixie, guys this is Josie." I say introducing everyone.

"I'm going to go on into the house, while you ladies catch up." Aunt Lucy says, then walks off.

"So, have you heard from Colby since he moved away? Josie asks.

I shake my head "No, we said we would text and call, but I guess he's busy."

"Forget boys, what's this UV party you mentioned on the phone?" Trixie questions.

Josie grins "A UV party here is really mental, ever seen the film Miss Congeniality?" She asks Trixie and she shakes her head. "Well, it's where everyone gets covered in UV paint, there's music blasting and it gets really messy. Also, it's a good place to meet cute boys," Josie says while hooking her one arm around my elbow and the other around Trixie's.

"Sounds like fun. Can't wait." Trixie says.

"Let's go up to my room for a bit and chill." I suggest and we all agree.

Opening my bedroom door, I jump on my bed.

"Oh my god how I have missed my bed," I say stretching out like a starfish. Trixie and Josie just stand there laughing.

"What? I can't help it if I miss my bed," I say then poke my tongue out at them.

Josie and Trixie sit either side of me on the bed, so I shuffle backwards and lean against the wall at the top.

"I am so jealous of you two, you're as close as sisters than best friends. I have nobody like that near where I live, all my friends live miles away," Trixie says.

"You should move down here. You've finished school, right? Why not transfer to the same college as JC" Josie suggests.

"Yeah Josie is right, you should transfer to the same one as me, St James's College."

Trixie glances between myself and Josie, "I don't know, I'll see how this weekend goes first." Trixie replies.

Josie's phone starts ringing, pulling it out of her jeans, she swipes the screen before answering.

"Hey Simon, yeah she's here. Hold on," she says then puts then phone on loudspeaker. "Go ahead Simon."

"JC, can you hear me?" Simon asks.

"Hey Simon, I'm here with Josie and my cousin Trixie." I reply.

"Hey Simon." Trixie adds.

"JC, Craig has been asking about you non-stop, will you go on a date with him?" he asks, there's no beating around the bush with him. I look across to Josie then at Trixie.

"Simon, I...."

Trixie cut me off, "Sorry Simon but you will have to match make with my cousin some other time, this weekend is a girls weekend only," she replies, then presses the end call button on Josie's phone.

"I cannot believe you hung up on him." Josie says. I just stare at Trixie.

"Well don't just stare at me like a goldfish with your mouth open wide. You were clearly lost for words, so I stepped in." Trixie explains.

"Thanks. I guess Colby is still on my mind, that's why I froze when he asked me about going on a date with Craig."

We spend the next few hours talking before getting ready for the UV party. Trixie has changed into a pair of denim, blue shorts, and black vest top. Josie borrowed a pair of black denim shorts and white vest top. I've changed into black leggings, a red vest top, pair it with my black sandals and small black bag. After taking a few selfie pics with Trixie and Josie, we head to the community centre.

Justin Timberlake's Can't Stop The Feeling blasts from the speakers and the disco lights flicker as we walk in the room. It's so busy with everyone dancing, paint is shooting from the all the corners of the room.

"Come on let's dance" Josie says, dragging me and Trixie into the middle of the room. The music changes to Shut Up And Dance by Walk The Moon.

"Oh my god I love this song." Trixie says and starts dancing like a crazy person.

"Me too" Josie agrees and joins her.

I laugh at them before a hand grabs mine and spins me around, it's Craig.

"Hey JC, dance with me." he says before grabbing the other hand. He pulls me into the crowd and we spent the next hour dancing while getting covered in paint. The song Despacito comes on and Craig stops dancing.

"Man, this is so freaking annoying, I hate this song. Do you want to go grab a drink?

I'm about to reply, when something catches my attention over his shoulder, a boy walks past. For a minute, I think it's Colby, but it can't be, he doesn't live around here.

"I'm sorry I can't, I have to go." I say, then go to find Josie and Trixie. I find them both dancing with Simon and some other boy I don't know.

"Hey guys, I'm going to head home, I'm not feeling to well," I lie.

"Oh JC, I'll come with you" Josie says, but Trixie cuts her off.

"No, you stay and enjoy the party, I'm tired, I'll take JC home,"

We say our goodbyes and walk home; I know Josie was excited for tonight, so I don't want to spoil her fun. It takes us twenty minutes to walk home. As we get to the front door the house opposite, lights turn on. I turn around and glance across the road and the lights go off again. Taking the key from my bag, I unlock the front door and walk in, Trixie follows closing the door behind her.

We head upstairs to my room, opening my door, I switch on the light before sitting in my chair, undo my sandal straps and take them off.

"So, what is really wrong? I don't buy that you don't feel well, so out with it. I'm family, you can tell me anything." Trixie says while kicking her wedge shoes off.

"Okay you're right. I felt fine when I was with Craig, he was asking me if I wanted to grab a drink, when I thought I saw Colby walking past. I guess I'm missing him so much that my mind is playing tricks on me. You probably think I am crazy."

Trixie walks over to me.

"No, I don't think you're crazy, I just think you are in love. However, I do think we look a right state." she says holding her arms out, looking herself up and down. We both laugh.

"Yeah think we should take a shower, but first let's take a photo." I say while grabbing my phone from in my paint covered bag. I snap a few pictures before jumping in the shower.

Chapter Thirteen

New Neighbours

A phone vibrating wakes me up, opening one eye, I glance on my bedside table to check my phone but its black. It must be Trixie's; my thoughts were right when she answers.

"Hello. Mmm, yeah two minutes," she answers to whoever she's talking to, then climbs out if bed and walks out the room, closing the door behind her.

Rolling over on to my stomach, I try to go back to sleep, but it's too late, I am wide awake. Giving up trying to go back to sleep, I decide to get up. Swinging the duvet back, I sit up on the edge of the bed with my feet dangling down. Grabbing my phone, I check the time, it's just gone seven-thirty, I swipe across the screen and check my notifications. Josie has tagged me in a few photos from the party last night, we look a right mess, all covered in paint. The bedroom door opens and Trixie walks back in.

"Who was calling you this early?" I ask.

She jumps on my bed, grinning like the cat in Alice In Wonderland.

"That was just Zeke, asking when we are going home. Let's go out for breakfast, you can show me around; Aunt Julie is still asleep, but mum is downstairs drinking coffee," she says then goes over to her bag, pulling out clothes.

"I'm going to get dressed, hurry up sleepy head. The sun is shining and the birds are tweeting, let's not waste the day away," she says, really cheerily, before going to the bathroom with her clothes to change.

Standing up, I walk across to my wardrobe and pull out my baby blue dress, and some clean underwear and change into them. I dig through my storage box, looking for my flat white, baby doll shoes. Just as I am slipping my feet in, my door opens.

"Come on, time waits for no man, let's go. Are you ready?" Trixie asks.

"Jesus Trix, where is the fire? Your eager to go out today. I just got to brush my hair, have a wash, then grab my purse, keys, and phone. Then I am ready." I tell her.

Twenty minutes later, we are sitting in a cafe in town, with scrambled egg on toast and a cup of tea.

"Have you seen your new neighbours that Josie mentioned yet?" Trixie asks before shovelling egg into her mouth.

"No, but apparently there is a cute boy moving in." I reply.

"So how would you feel if you saw Colby and Ross again?" she asks.

Placing my fork on the table I look at her, she's been acting weird since she had the phone call this morning.

"Probably be surprised. Okay I give up what are you hiding, you been acting really weird since you got off the phone with Zeke." I say, staring at her suspiciously.

"I don't know what you mean, nothing's going on." she replies, glancing across the room.

"So, what will you do when you go back home, now that the Ryan boys don't live next door?" I ask changing the subject.

Her phone chooses that moment to ring. She takes it out of her bag then answers.

"Hello, oh hey Ross. No, I'm not home me and mum are with JC and Aunt Julie. We are staying until tomorrow, yeah Zeke told me…" she pauses and smiles listening to whatever he's saying. "Yeah, I won't, I promise. I'll speak to you soon, bye," she says then hangs up.

"What was that about? Have you spoken to him since they moved?"

"Yeah, a few times, he's pretty busy unpacking the new place. Come on let's go grab a film," she suggests.

We finish our drinks then pay for breakfast, before making our way to the cinema. Josie calls when we were on the way over and wants to join. We miss the eleven o'clock film while we wait for her to turn up. Checking my phone again for the third time in a space of ten minutes, I swipe across about to dial Josie's number, when she appears in front of us.

"Sorry I'm late, I got talking to Simon on the phone." she explains.

"Come on let's go get our tickets and snacks for Mamma Mia Two." Trixie suggests.

We line up to get our tickets and snacks, then join the queue to go in.

Two hours and forty minutes later, and we are walking out if the cinema.

"That was amazing." Trixie says.

"I love that film; I was a massive fan of the first one, but I think I enjoyed that more," I say, but Josie butts in.

"You're crazy, I loved the first one better, I did love all the songs in the second one though," she adds.

When we manage to get outside the cinema, it's still busy with it being the six weeks holidays. All the parents are taking their kids to see the latest Hotel Transylvania Three film.

"Let's go next door to the bowling alley and see if we can book a lane." Trixie suggests.

"Oh yes, let's make it a full girlie weekend. Bowling and we could play pool as well." Josie agrees.

"Sure, why not, I'll text mum to let her know where we are." I tell them as I take my phone out of my bag and send a text, before placing it back in my bag.

We walk up to the help desk and Trixie starts talking to the woman behind the counter.

"Hi, I was wondering if you have any lanes available for the bowling?" she asks.

"Hi, yes we have one free in about half hour." The woman replies.

"Awesome, can I book it please, the name is Jodi Collins." Trixie tells the woman before paying.

"We will call you on the overhead speakers." The woman explains, then Trixie thanks her.

"Well we have half hour to kill, so let's go play some pool," she says and we head over to the pool tables, near the bar area in the Bowlplex.

"Here you go set the balls up, I need the toilet." I say giving Josie money for the pool table. My phone vibrates in my bag, I pull it out, it's just mum replying to my text.

Have fun sweetie x

I put it back in my bag and use the toilet, and wash my hands, before going back out to find the girls. When I find them, they are not alone, Simon and Craig are talking to them. *Josie the little witch, she invited, them I curse inside.*

"Hey JC, look who just turned up" Josie says beaming. I frown at her, but quickly hide it.

"We going to play tag team, winners stay on myself and Craig against you and Josie." Trixie explains.

"I'm sitting this round out," Simon adds.

"Actually, you four can play, I have to reply to a message." I say.

I don't want to give Craig any ideas, so, I sit on a chair and pretend to text while they play. Craig keeps looking my way when he thinks I'm not looking. Just as Simon and Josie are down to their last yellow ball, my name is called.

JODIE COLLINS YOUR LANE IS NOW READY. THAT'S JODIE COLLINS TO LANE SIX.

Putting my phone away I jump up," I'll go set the lane up," I say and start walking across to the lane.

"Yo, JC, mind if we play?" Simon yells.

"Sure, why not." I reply.

I'm seriously going to throttle Josie later.

Trixie runs up to me as I am setting the lane up.

"JC relax, have fun. You won't be left alone with Craig, I promise," she whispers in my ear.

"Fine, let's bowl." I reply.

We spend the next hour bowling, Trixie kept her promise and she never left me alone with Craig. The boys walked with us back to my house, before walking Josie to hers.

"Hey mum we are home," I shout while opening the door.

"We are in the kitchen," mum shouts back.

Trixie closes the door as we walk into the kitchen.

"You girls have fun today?" Aunt Lucy asks, while mixing a brown mixture in a bowl, while Mum's stirring something in a saucepan on the cooker.

"Wow, you guys are busy. Are we expecting company?" I ask, taking a seat at the table.

"Yes, I invited the new neighbours around for dinner, to welcome them to the neighbourhood." Mum replies, smiling.

"Something smells yummy, what are you cooking Aunt Julie?" Trixie asks, walking over to the cooker for a nosey.

"I'm making creamy lamb curry with a hint of coconut in it and pilau rice and I have garlic naan breads to go in the oven as well. Food won't be ready for a while yet. Why don't you go upstairs for a bit and relax in your room," mum suggests.

"Sure, sounds like a good idea, I can kick your bum on Mario kart." Trixie says.

"Yeah you wish. Mum what time are the new neighbours coming over?" I ask, while standing up.

"I told them to come over for six, so you have plenty of time."

"What are they like, the new neighbours? Josie said there is a boy around my age, have you seen him?" I ask.

She laughs, "Yes JC, I have seen him, he helped us bring the shopping in earlier. Nice young man, but I think he is a few years older than you. You'll meet him and his mother later," she explains before glancing at Aunt Lucy, then turns back around to stir the curry.

We spend the next three hours playing on the Nintendo Wii, Trixie is on a winning streak, when mum tells me to get changed into something more suitable before the neighbours arrive.

"JC, would you pop to the shop for me please, I forgot to get some ice cream to go with the chocolate fudge cake," mum shouts from downstairs.

"Sure, I'll be there now," I reply and walk downstairs, leaving Trixie playing solo on Mario Kart against the computer.

Grabbing the money, I head out to the shop around the corner for the vanilla ice cream. It doesn't take me long, and I'm back within ten minutes, opening the door, I shout, "Mum I'm back." Walking in to the kitchen, I put the ice cream in the freezer and give mum her change, just as the doorbell rings.

"I'll get it," Trixie chirps before walking off towards the front door.

"Aunt Lucy, do you know what's going on with Trixie today, she's been acting really weird?" I pause when I hear voices. I know that voice, I turn around just as Trixie returns with Ross and Mrs Ryan behind her.

"Hi come in, have a seat, you will have to excuse daughter I think she has lost her manners. This is JC." Mum smiles introducing me.

"Nice to see you again JC," Mrs Ryan says.

I nod and glance at Ross.

"You look like you've just seen a ghost," he says before pulling me in for a hug. I tense, when I notice the person behind him, Colby.

"JC, I know you are happy to see me and all, but could you not squeeze the life out of me," Ross joke's.

"Let's all take a seat, dinner is ready to serve, JC, why don't you give me a hand, while your mum sits down with Chloe and the boys." Aunt Lucy suggests and I quickly scarper to the corner of kitchen, hidden from sight, without saying a word to Colby.

My heart is racing so fast, it feels like it's going to come out of my chest.

"JC, your mum had no clue who Colby was when she invited him and his family over for dinner. I know it was a shock but..."

I cut her off. "I can't breathe my heart is going too fast."

I start panicking. Colby comes around the corner, Aunt Lucy steps to the side. He comes closer cupping my face with both his hands, leaning his forehead against mine.

"I'm going to take these over to the table," Lucy says.

"Jodi, listen to me baby. Close your eyes breathe in, then slowly out. Keep doing it, breathe in and out," he says quietly.

My heart feels like it's slowing back to normal and I can breathe again.

"Jodi can you look at me?" He asks after a few minutes; I open my eyes and he's gazing back at me. "There's my beautiful girl," he says then kisses my forehead.

"Excuse me, I hate to interrupt, it's all cute you found each other again, but I am kind of getting hungry. So, can we save the reunion until after we eat, "Trixie teases.

Colby laughs, moving backwards glancing at her.

"Heaven forbid we get in the way of you and chocolate," he replies.

Moving around him, I feel a little less tense after the shock of seeing him. I carry the naan breads and take a seat at the table, opposite Mrs Ryan. Trixie follows, carrying the rice and Colby is behind her holding the big serving dish with the curry in. Then they both take a seat the other side of the table.

"Everyone help yourselves." Mum says, then starts placing some rice on her plate. Everyone else follows her.

"This is delicious Julie, thank you again for inviting us over. You will have to come over to ours sometime, when we have unpacked everything," Mrs Ryan suggests.

"Your welcome and we would love to come over when you are more settled. JC, you didn't mention you already know Chloe and her sons," Mum says in between eating her curry.

I start coughing and Ross taps me on the back.

"Thanks. I didn't know they were our new neighbours. When I was staying with Aunt Lucy, I spent most of the time on the beach or by the pool at Mrs Ryan's house with Trixie, Zeke Colby and Ross." I explain.

"Well mostly with Colby." Ross adds.

I kicked him under the table, glaring at him, my cheeks start to burn and I am sure I look like a ripe tomato.

"Trixie and Zeke were there too," I try to say.

"Chloe, you are a sly little bird you never said you were moving down this way. We're going to miss you living next door," Aunt Lucy says changing the subject.

"I know it happened to fast, when we found out I got the new job in the office in town. I guess fate brought us here for a reason." Mrs Ryan replies and smiles at me.

Chapter Fourteen

The Kiss

Sitting on my bed reading, while Trixie is still asleep, it's no surprise she's still out cold. She spent ages last night talking to Ross on the phone, then talked my ears off about him, until early hours this morning. I didn't talk much to Colby last night, every time we tried to talk; I could feel eyes watching us.

Mum kept a close eye on me after she learnt I spent most of my summer with Colby, thanks to Ross's little confession. I'm still shocked they are living directly opposite us. Just when I thought I might take a chance with Craig; the boy whole stole my heart appears. As crazy as it sounds, I think our fate is written in the stars.

There is a knock on the door before it opens, its Aunt Lucy.

"Morning sweetie, I guess someone's tired this morning," she says motioning to Trixie, before coming over and sitting on the edge of the bed.

"While sleeping beauty's still asleep I wanted to have a chat to you before we leave today. I know you were shocked when you saw Colby last night at dinner. Don't hide your feelings for him sweetheart, open your heart and let him in. I've never seen him like the way he was with you last night." She says, then kisses me on the side of the head. "Trixie, you need to wake up, we will be leaving after breakfast."

"Nooo, too tired need to sleep," she says and pulls the duvet over her head.

"Well you shouldn't have stayed up all night talking, now shift your bum Missy," Aunt Lucy says while she yanks the duvet from Trixie.

"You're mean," she moans and sits up rubbing the sleep from her eyes.

"Well you can sleep in the car; I'm taking us all out for breakfast and I want to pop over the road to see Chloe before we go as well." Aunt Lucy says before dropping the duvet on the floor and walking back out of the room.

Once the door closes, Trixie flops backwards onto the bed.

"Why couldn't she just let me sleep ten minutes longer, he was about to kiss me," she says.

"Huh. He who?" I ask feeling lost.

"Ross, I was in his arms, he was so close and then Grrrr, mum woke me up," she whines throwing her arm over her face dramatically.

"Well you could actually kiss him in real life and not just in your dreams." I tease her.

Trixie springs up, "You know that isn't such a bad idea," she says, before jumping up and running around the room, gathering her clothes chucking them into a bag like a crazy person. I fall backwards onto the bed laughing.

"Trixie, are you planning on going to breakfast in your pyjamas?" I ask, in between laughing.

She pauses and stares at me," Balls can I borrow something of yours to wear? I have nothing cute," she says giving me puppy dog eyes.

"Sure, let's go find something before Aunt Lucy comes in with a cup of cold water to throw over you." I climb off the bed and hunt for clothes for both of us to wear.

Thirty minutes later we are both dressed, Trixie wearing my blue denim shorts and white black vest top with her sandals. I decided on my black denim three quarter jeans, with a white tank top and trainers. We set off to have breakfast at a cafe in town.

After breakfast we head home, it was nice seeing mum have someone to talk to, she must be lonely since dad passed away. Just as we pull up outside, I notice Ross in the garden talking on his phone, his appearance doesn't go unnoticed by Trixie either. Aunt Lucy turns the engine off and we all climb out.

"I am going to see Chloe before we pack the car up," she says and walks over the road.

Mum walks up to the house, unlocking the front door and me and Trixie follow her in.

"Well I better go get my things from upstairs," Trix says before disappearing, leaving just me and mum alone.

"JC, I want to say that I am so proud of you and your dad would be too. You have turned in to a beautiful young lady." Mum says, then wraps her arms around me in a hug.

I squeeze her back, "Thank you mum, I love you."

"Love you too baby," she adds just as the front door opens and Aunt Lucy walks in.

"Ross just said Chloe and Colby have gone onto town and won't be back until after dinner. Where has Trixie gone?" she asks just as Trixie walks down the stairs

"Right here mum, I just got my things from upstairs."

"Okay sweetie, can you say goodbye to your cousin and Aunt Julie, then put your things in the car. I need to go grab my charger and bag from upstairs." Aunt Lucy says before walking upstairs.

"It was lovely having you stay for a few days, anytime you want to come back for a visit you are always welcome," Mum says to Trixie.

"Thanks Aunt Julie, I will definitely be back," she replies.

Hooking my arm through Trixie's, I tell her, "I'll walk out to the car with you."

She opens the car boot and chucks her bag in, leaving the it open for Aunt Lucy. Trix keeps looking across the street at Ross, who is still on the phone.

"Trix, remember our fate is written in the stars, if it's meant to be, you will find each other again," I say just as mum and Aunt Lucy come from nowhere.

"Find who?" Aunt Lucy asks closing the car boot.

"Never mind Mum," Trixie says and walks to the passenger door opening it. My aunt walks up to me, giving me a goodbye hug and does the same to Mum.

"Next time we won't leave it so long," she says and waves to Ross, who is now watching.

"Tell your mum I will phone her," she shouts and he nods in acknowledgement.

"Are you ready to go Trixie?" Aunt Lucy asks as she walks around to the driver's side, opening the door.

"You know what Mum, no, there is one more thing I need to do. It's now or never." Trixie mutters before walking past me and mum, across the street to where Ross is. Pulling his shirt forward, she kisses him while he's on the phone. He drops it on the floor and cups her face with both hands, before she lets go of him.

"Call me," she says and winks, before walking back across the street and climbs into the car, shutting the door after her.

"Well didn't see that one coming," Aunt Lucy says with surprise in her voice. She then climbs in and starts the engine, before reversing, to turn the car around and drives off with a beep on the horn.

It's not long before they are out of sight, I glance across the street and Ross is still standing there with his mouth wide open.

I'd say she's finally shocked him; I laugh and hook my arm with Mums and walk into the house. We decide to do something we haven't done together for a long while and spend the afternoon making cakes together.

The house has been quiet without Trixie, she was the life of the party. With her gone and Josie spending all her time with Simon, I began to reconnect with mum. Having Aunt Lucy and Trixie stay with us, brought us closer together again.

After dad died, we drifted apart, but now things are getting back to the way things used to be. We spent four hours in the kitchen, making cakes and pies, before watching the old films, Top Gun and Ghost on the sofa.

Just as Ghost was coming to the end there's a knock on the door.

"I'll get it," Mum says walking over to the front door. The door opens and closes. I press pause on the film and turn around to ask who it is, when she walks in with Colby behind her.

"I think I am going to have an early night," she says and walks over to me and kisses me on the head. "Listen to your heart," she whispers, before saying goodnight to Colby and goes upstairs.

"Hi." I say.

He smirks," Mind if I join you?" he asks.

I shake my head.

"What are you watching?" he asks as he takes his jacket off before sitting on the sofa.

"It's Ghost, but I can turn it off if you don't want to watch it." I say.

He chuckles, "Nah, leave it on there's about half hour left. I've seen it before."

I glance at him with wide eyes, "Oh." I say.

"It was when Trixie went through that breakup. We did anything we could to cheer her up and one of the things was to sit down and watch a pile of chick films," he explains further.

"You are sweet." I tell him.

Thirty minutes later, and the credits are rolling, glancing to the side, I notice that Colby is watching me.

"Remember when we went up on the top of that cliff, overlooking the beach and we watched the stars?" he asks.

"Yeah the sky was so clear you could see loads of stars." I reply.

"Let's go outside and see if we can find Orion's belt," he suggests, while standing up and holds his hand out.

Taking his hand, we walk out to the back garden, the sky is only just starting to go dark.

"I don't think it's dark enough yet to see the stars."

"Yeah give it twenty minutes for it do go darker then we should be able to see them. While we wait, how about a dance," he asks, taking his phone out and swiping across it a few times. Before placing the phone on the small metal table, that was leaning against the wall, under the kitchen window. Music starts playing and I recognised the song, it's Unchained Melody, the song from Ghost.

Taking me by both hands, he pulls me with him further out into the garden then holds me close, as we move to the music. I close my eyes laying my head on his chest, I feel contented and the most relaxed I have felt in a long time. Everything and everyone else are a blur.

"Jodi look," Colby says, shaking me out of my comfort zone.

The music has stopped and I gaze up into the sky, the stars are now visible. I can see Orion's belt like the first time Colby showed me.

"I guess you can see certain stars from anywhere in the world. It's beautiful." I say while gazing up at the sky.

"Not as beautiful as you. Jodi Collins will you be my girl?" he asks, looking at me.

"Colby you had me from the moment our eyes met, our fate was written in the stars. My heart belongs to you." I say gazing into his eyes.

"The stars aligned and brought me you. You had me under a spell the moment our eyes met. You are my girl Jodi," he says as he cups my face, leans in and kisses me on the lips. I completely melt into him.

He slowly pulls back, and says, "I have wanted to do that all summer," before he kisses me again taking my breath away.

The End

Sun, Sea & Boys

L.M. Evans

Author Bio

L.M Evans is a kitchen assistant living in South Wales with her husband and three children, she enjoys going for long walks in the countryside with her family and going to the movies.

When she's not busy running around after her children you'll either find her working on her blog, BLOGL.MEVANS. Writing or reading one of her favourite books.

In 2011 after a friend suggested she should write her own book.
She decided to write her first book called Ryder James. She published it in December 2014 and she never looked back. Ryder James has since been revamped and is now under the new title Starstruck.

Sun, Sea & Boys

L.M. Evans

Contact Author

Facebook
https://www.facebook.com/AUTHORL.MEVANS/

Twitter
@Louisem07021983 https://twitter.com/Louisem07021983?s=09

Instagram
Louisem070283

Blog Facebook Page
https://www.facebook.com/BLOGLMEVANS

Blog
https://louisemarieevans.blogspot.co.uk/?m=1&zx=50bb660e29 3dfa01

Sun, Sea & Boys

Printed in Poland
by Amazon Fulfillment
Poland Sp. z o.o., Wrocław